The S II

'Assignation'

by
Andrew David Doyle

iUniverse, Inc.
Bloomington

The Silent Apostle II
'Assignation'

Copyright © 2013 by Andrew David Doyle.

All rights reserved. No part of this book may be used or reproduced by any means, graphic, electronic, or mechanical, including photocopying, recording, taping or by any information storage retrieval system without the written permission of the publisher except in the case of brief quotations embodied in critical articles and reviews.

iUniverse books may be ordered through booksellers or by contacting:

iUniverse
1663 Liberty Drive
Bloomington, IN 47403
www.iuniverse.com
1-800-Authors (1-800-288-4677)

Because of the dynamic nature of the Internet, any web addresses or links contained in this book may have changed since publication and may no longer be valid. The views expressed in this work are solely those of the author and do not necessarily reflect the views of the publisher, and the publisher hereby disclaims any responsibility for them.

Any people depicted in stock imagery provided by Thinkstock are models, and such images are being used for illustrative purposes only.
Certain stock imagery © Thinkstock.

ISBN: 978-1-4759-6585-8 (sc)
ISBN: 978-1-4759-6586-5 (ebk)

Printed in the United States of America

iUniverse rev. date: 12/07/2012

Contents

Author's Preface to the First Edition vii

Chapter One	The Priory Warnings	1
Chapter Two	Epitaph	23
Chapter Three	A brush with the law	38
Chapter Four	Cairo	42
Chapter Five	'The Disappearing Chalice'	55
Chapter Six	The Assignation of Worlds	64
Chapter Seven	Malta	102
Chapter Eight	A date with death	105
Chapter Nine	Human Emotion	114
Chapter Ten	The Grand Lodge of Cairo	121
Chapter Eleven	The Vatican Responds	129
Chapter Twelve	Womanly Charms	131
Chapter Thirteen	Tartarus Inferni	137

Afterword 163

Author's Preface to the First Edition

This particular edition has not been exposed to the pending audience and will undoubtedly become another object of desire for any serious science/biblical fiction reader. Any misunderstanding or misinterpretation are purely intentional and a luxury that is afforded to the fantasy fiction writer.

I have, in certain accounts from the varying sources, condensed such detail and information so as not to cloud the work by overwhelming, analytical detail that often lurks behind simplicity and study—especially in such subjects as mythology and subject matter relating to the church, both of which are complicated in their own right.

The lapse of nearly a quarter century since writing the original scripts for this edition has called for many alterations to the accounts of the later condition of information availability. Therefore, I have not departed from the original scope of the work.

The list of hidden contributors from web searches and other sources consulted and used as applications,

Andrew David Doyle

coupled with the personal visits to most places that I have been required to make, will show that the labour bestowed in bringing out this project has not been slight and is cited as such for this work.

Chapter One
The Priory Warnings

Noun—'*Assignation*'—a clandestine—meeting or tryst.

The squeal and screech of the warm tyres on the warm tarmac was almost unbearable to the ears as the red flash of the Jaguar skidded passed and beyond the wooden gates to the old Scottish graveyard. The huge mass of the machine could be seen sliding easily along the soft tarmac by a good 20 feet as the driver wrestled with the controls as the car skidded from left to right to avoid the man standing in its travel path.

Kemp Hastings had hit the brake pedal with so much force that he could almost feel the pressure of the hydraulic oil travel up his right leg and deep into his unsuspecting groin: an instant reaction of his body in relation to the sudden appearance of someone or something which had quite simply and unceremoniously stepped into the middle of the roadway catching him unawares.

Kemp would normally navigate these leafy lanes like a rally driver on heat as a matter of course and knew every twist and turn on the rural speed track, as this would be his little escape as he battled with rules and regulations imposed upon him for road users in the back drop of rural Scotland.

His escape would be exercised on most occasions as he sped through the back roads and country lanes of Angus, an enriched part of Scotland, whilst releasing his anger and frustrations for a few brief seconds in his protests of heavy costs and very bad automobile service. Of course always, remaining mindful that the odd animal, such as a deer or a sheep, which had, on occasions, wandered on to the roadway. Or on one occasion, a stag had leapt the fencing and surprised him, and may actually surprise him still.

But this event was something entirely different. It wasn't every day that a person wandered deliberately into one's travel path. This vision was certainly not an animal and it was not a clump of grass or a shadow. This unsuspecting figure added a whole new dimension to his physical reaction speed times towards avoiding the apparition which was, as far as Hastings was concerned, that his responses were spot on perfect. And he had hit the brakes within a hundredth of a gnat's bollock nana second on spying the person.

This single event somehow sent a sudden, cold fear propelling up through his shocked, grey matter; momentarily catching his senses totally off guard and unawares, forcing him to make a split second decision—a decision where such lightning-quick reactions to such events had cost and saved many lives in the past.

It was that moment in time where Kemp had taken a very deep breath. Just seconds before the asbestos abrasive coating of the brake pads gripped the stainless steel discs of the ABS braking system, momentarily sending a series of incredible jolts up through the body of the car and deep into Hastings's lower spine.

A strong series of sporadic pulses that had technically brought the crimson beast to an almost controlled mechanical halt as the forward momentum of force began hurling his unsuspecting body forwards into the smooth beige leather seat. Then, simultaneously sending his upper body headlong towards the soft cladding of the steering wheel.

Hastings had been propelled so far forward that he bumped his face against the rim of the steering wheel, cutting his upper lip in the process. That was before being hurled violently backwards in the opposite direction, almost ripping the muscles in the back of his neck apart.

Time had also frozen momentarily as the spiritual and phenomenal detective momentarily sat backwards in the driving seat for the second time, having fought with the padded bulge of the car driver's airbag: the life-saving appliance strategically hidden within the confines of the steering wheel itself.

Having wrestled with the steering wheel for several seconds with all his strength and skills, as any mature driver normally would, he was struggling in order to bring the car to a controlled halt. It was then that the air bag fully popped out of its housing and deployed itself in a haze of fluff and the release of pressurised air—coupled with a high pitch whine and almost smothering him in the process.

Another very deep breath and he gazed into the rear view mirror, still wrestling with the airbag. He was expecting to see a body strewn over the black tarmac roadway, albeit he recalled that he had heard no bumps or thumps, and had been psychologically preparing himself to have witnessed a twelve to fourteen stone person first being struck by the front bumper. Yet, to his astonishment the figure was still standing there, and scarily was staring whilst pointing back at him.

"Shit! This is not good," he exclaimed, softly.

The car itself could have had easily become an insurance write off and things for him, physically, could have been much worse by far if he had not been so alert at the time the stranger had suddenly stepped out of the Chapel gates and on to the roadway.

Never-the-less, he succumbed to the fact that his precious, little red car had suffered extensive damage and his seat belt had perhaps saved his life. And yet, he was somehow supposed to be grateful.

He was correct in his assumption in that he had in fact missed the figure completely. And he was somewhat relieved at the same time, but, not exactly sure what he had expected. Especially during the critical moments prior to contact; then a moment of nothing, followed by a very uneasy, cold fear.

He stopped and paused for thought again. He was half prepared to experience the body of a person being hurled over the bonnet and up onto the windscreen of the car, ending up in a sprawled mass of blood, shit and feathers across the tarmac road—not unlike a deer or fox.

"No way can this happen," he muttered again softly under his breath. Then he began to exit the Jaguar.

Stepping out of the car, he took another glance back up the roadway. Then stared aimlessly at his handy work, thinking that, potentially, he could have flipped the soft top over completely, which would have been almost fatal.

He then thought hard about having to peel the heather and the clumps of wet, green grass and foliage from his mirrors and from inside the cockpit, had he rolled the one and a half ton vehicle over, let alone observe what may still be a dead or very injured person. He was relieved of course that he did not have to. He smirked inwardly, then thought again about what might have been. Shrugging his shoulders, he stood fully upright.

"Ouch! Oh, cack, that's not good!" he cried, then coughed, which was followed by a few more small, muscular cricks and twitches from his spine and lower back. And he reckoned he was in good shape—well in good enough condition—that was whilst considering the force of the impact of the machine as it was rammed up against the stone wall.

Then considering his state of being having observed and acknowledged the amount of damage the car had actually sustained, he gave himself another internal 'well done' for having brought the vehicle to a well-controlled stop under extreme conditions and not killing himself, and he gazed on.

"Well, that's not going to be cheap," he muttered away to himself, and snorted whilst wiping his brow, simultaneously flicking open his mobile telephone and staring back up the roadway to where the figure had been previously standing. He then glanced over toward the churchyard and gazed directly at the tall, tower walls of the medieval keep of the Priory building that dominated the foreground.

The blood on his lip had started to trickle down on to his chin and had already stained his new blue and red chequered countryside 'Fruit of the Loom' shirt, leaving a tiny trickle of DNA for all to see.

It was then, that he momentarily became very uncomfortable and somewhat confused as he could not make head or tail of what he had really just witnessed. The car accident was real enough but the circumstances leading up to the event were pretty much inexplicable as far as he was concerned, even for a man of his educational standing.

He then began walking nearer to where the figure had stood. He was hoping to find some sort of clue to the odd event, although he was consciously glancing to his left and right side as he walked, half expecting to find a deranged druid lurking in the nearby bushes, potentially waiting to jump out from the hedge line and mug him.

After three steps or so he began to talk into the mouthpiece of his cell phone. "Hello, can you hear me? Anybody out there? Hello it's me, Kemp."

He heard nothing apart from incoherent mumblings and ramblings coming from the earpiece on his mobile. He stopped and listened intently trying to decipher what sounded to him like a range of gargles and burbles coming from a three year old child in the background.

Several moments later he dropped the phone down by his side on hearing what he thought was another vehicle approaching from the near distance. It was then that the battery on his mobile telephone decided to die, and it bleeped three times just to let him know that it had had enough activity for the time being.

"Piece of cack! I thought those bloody batteries lasted more than six hours."

Stepping off the roadway and onto the soft grassy verge, he waited and watched with the intention of grabbing the attention of a passing driver and to find an opportunity to ask for assistance. He even considered asking for a lift back to the village, as opposed to just locking the car up and going for a brisk walk to his home.

He also considered asking for a tow to his home just a few miles away, or conversely, if he should just call the police and get a lift home from them. Well, he would call them if his damn phone had retained its bloody charge.

Kicking a stone underfoot, he started making his way back to his car, and he sauntered by the chapel gateway where he stopped and took another long glance at the Priory's tall steeple tower. He thought he had just caught sight of a figure standing in one of the tower's higher windows.

But he dismissed this as an optical illusion because of the weather conditions and a trick of the morning light. His peripheral vision was normally very keen, but he remained mindful that he had just taken a bit of a knock during the incident.

He also knew that to find anyone standing in the tower was clearly impossible as the stairwell up the tall tower was long gone and pretty much destroyed in the tower's volatile history.

And primarily due to the fact that he had visited the Priory so often that he, on one occasion, had tried to scale the outer wall himself. But to no avail: apart from scraped fingers and a bruised knee whilst destroying a rather nice pair of chino denim trousers. Any notion of a figure in the window was quite absurd and out of the question.

He momentarily spied the underneath of the machine and acknowledged to himself that it was totally mangled. The hydraulic piping appeared to be okay but the plastic and metal cowling that covered in and around the offside light cluster was severely cracked with the lens and housing literally destroyed. He then spied a few droplets of what he thought was hydraulic oil on the greenery.

He was more than pissed off that a long, hairline crack had appeared across the top left wheel arch and the new front alloy wheels had suffered severe damage and scathing. He knew that it would require careful repair or replacement.

But all in all he knew it wasn't going to break the bank completely—after all that's what insurances are for. But still, Jaguars do cost a fortune to maintain, and he reminded himself that his ego had been somewhat tarnished. Although he was still very annoyed with himself but he still managed a smile.

The car was possibly driveable or so he thought. Just as the oncoming car approached the scene of where the black tyre skid marks had started. Kemp could see the four way hazard warning lights had started to flash on the car and that was when he flipped his phone closed and stepped off the grass verge.

The oncoming driver was already alerted to the scene before her, and had taken safety steps and had parked her vehicle nearer the grassy embankment. The car had pulled up against the verge a good ten metres or so away—just as Kemp turned and placed a hand on the bonnet of his damaged sports car. Then he nonchalantly stared into the open green fields that stretched out before him.

He took another glimpse back at the motorist to find, to his further astonishment, that his friend and colleague Dr Darlene Gammay had emerged from the driver's seat and was walking briskly toward him.

"Hello, Kemp, how's tricks?" she said, in an almost smuggish, cynical way.

"Can't say that I am surprised to see you hanging around yet another church yard," she muttered softly, observing the awkward angle of the crashed car, which was propped up hard against the stone curtain wall that ran the length of the boneyard.

"And what an odd way to park your bonnie wee car."

Kemp was obviously annoyed, especially as his ego had been bruised, and only compounded more so by Darlene finding him at his most vulnerable. Hastings blinked his eyes several times, he wiped his face again, shook his head sideways and then responded in a relatively well-controlled manner.

"Not now, Darlene, please. I have just skidded half the length of this bloody road. Right from over there to away down over here, and I am a bit annoyed to say the least . . . Well, you know what I mean, and if I did not possess the reactions of a jet fighter pilot, I could have easily ended up simply slushed and pulped under the weight of my own car, and that would have ruined my chinos completely," he replied, pointing to the tarmac road as it stretched back to where the signpost was sitting at an odd angle, partially obscured by the overhanging branches of the tree line. He tried simultaneously to raise a smile.

"Mmm, Kemp, not sure being a jet fighter pilot would have saved you from the undergrowth. Though, maybe you would need to be more of a fairground dodgem car driver—now that particular skill would best fit. But, really are you okay? You do look a little bit flushed to me," she asked, as a concerned friend.

"You whizzed passed me about five miles back toward Brechin. I tried catching you up, but you took off like a Scouser at a police convention, a certain red bat out of hell. And I see you must have lost it on the corner then?"

She leaned forward and turned to look at the front of the car. Meanwhile, Hastings took a good look at Darlene's slender, rear end as she bent over the bonnet of the vehicle to inspect the damage.

It was not the first time he had been distracted by her womanly charms especially when presented with high end clothing attached. It was then that she spied his lecherous, boyish gaze, and smiled back at him. Then as she momentarily stared into his eyes, she flippantly remarked, "I hope it is in better shape than your front end is, Mister Hastings!"

Darlene was clad in a retro 1950's outfit: a black Coco Chanel pinafore dress with matching scarf and gloves. She wore classy and black sensible Jimmy Choo shoes and looked every part the biblical studies Professor that she was.

Hastings momentarily smiled and thought that Jackie Onassis would not look out of place standing next to his new partner, and he inwardly smiled, harbouring the thought that he might himself come to a sticky end.

He then motioned her to see if they could, together, free the heavy car from the grappling undergrowth. And, after several minutes of vehicular jostling, both cars were parked up in the small car park nearer to the Priory. Darlene sat next to Kemp in the Jaguar. Then picked her moment to speak, "You look a little pale, Kemp, that jolt might have given you a hidden injury or something."

Hastings coughed and leaned forwards toward the Doctor, then explained what he thought had happened, "Darlene, you are most probably correct. But you must listen to this, there was actually someone standing bang in the middle of the road—I swear it. I know I should have mowed them down like a mouse in a wheat field trying to escape a combine harvester, but I missed them completely or they were just not there. Maybe I was hallucinating, I do not know. The person should have emerged like crinkle cut chips having passed through the cheese grater grill on this machine.

And I know there was nowhere to run, as I was travelling at nearly forty five miles an hour. But, here is the funny thing, I drove straight through him, her or it. I am sure it was the figure of man standing directly in front of my car, and he was positioned right in the middle of the bloody road. Darlene, he materialised from nowhere, and he, she or it, was there for a full three to five seconds before I . . ."

Kemp cut off his dialogue and took a moment to pause for contemplative thought before speaking again. "Darlene, it was a Grey Friar Monk and that much I am pretty certain of. Shit, I have spent more time talking to them recently than I have talking with my own Mum."

Darlene crunched her hair up in a quick bun, and flicked a few curls from her eye line. "Okay, I do believe you, all things being equal and all that pretentious poppycock," she replied, having applied her specific kind of logic, and more importantly given her recent biblical experience. She knew she could talk to Hastings about most things—herself having had a bit of experience and authority in the given subject matter.

"These inexplicable things do happen, goodness, and, you have probably had more exposure and seen more than your fair share of odd and inexplicable occurrences, and weird and wonderful experiences than most professionals have," she said, whilst remaining informed about the nature of Kemp's complicated investigative world, just before she posed another question.

"Do you think this might have anything to do with my new tattoo? Or maybe, like me, you're just a little bit stressed because of circumstances at the moment? Kemp, you said yourself these things slowly chip away at you and can just creep up un-noticed and build up to a point, where sphlaaatt you are knackered," she implied then stroked his forehead flicking a few loose strands of his thick head of sandy brown hair back into place.

She then found a tissue and wiped the residue of dried blood from his upper lip and chin. "That's much better; you don't look like a dodgy vampire now. I think you had best get the quack to give you the once over though, you never know with car incidents you may feel okay now, but in a week's time or so you could fall over with a broken rib or ruptured something, and could develop into a far more worse condition. I have taken the liberty and sent a text to a police friend of mine to inform him you clipped the verge and no other person was involved—there is no reason to complicate things anymore than they already are . . ."

Hastings glanced over her right shoulder and smirked. "Thanks, I have absolutely no idea," he replied, and turned the ignition key. "Coffee," he muttered. Then he asked Darlene to follow him.

"No wait Kemp, before you go, do you think this is a good idea to drive? And you do have to ask yourself will this nice machine actually make it? I mean, after all, it is only a bloody car, it could have some sort of hidden hydraulic damage—you know, brake pipes, clutch that kind of thing. There is absolutely no sense in tempting fate again, now is there? C'mon, I'll drive you home, how does that sound?" she offered.

Hastings thought for a second then agreed with Darlene's logic and removed the ignition keys. Then grabbing his brown leather satchel from the rear seat, he exited and locked the Jaguar and jumped into the passenger seat of Darlene's Range Rover.

"Cannot drive with an airbag like that anyway," he said.

Darlene smiled back at him, then drove more slowly than she normally would have, especially through the back roads and lanes in that part of the country, where mindless, city dwellers would use the back roads as racing tracks. And, of course, Kemp was testament to that statement, albeit the Range Rover was too big to throw around the tight lanes, too many tractors for Darlene's liking.

She flicked the interior mirror forward then thought about a way to distract him from his recent trauma, then she spoke, "I received a parcel in the post yesterday, and you will never guess in a million years what it was." She posed the question in a more relaxed, jovial kind of way, still trying to keep the subject matter away from the macabre and the recent car accident.

Hastings pursed his lips waited for a second or two then nodded his head slowly from left to right then spoke. "It's not our stolen Dante oil painting by any chance is it?"

Darlene was momentarily dumbstruck and just stared aimlessly straight back at him at first, then, stared way out beyond the passenger window gazing well into the far distant horizon, somehow avoiding to crash the car in the process. "How the hell in God's name did you manage to guess that," she exclaimed, whilst abruptly flicking her mobile phone shut. Then she pressed the blue button on the disk player to play.

"C'mon Darlene, I was only joking, it was a wild, educated guess. Look at things this way: with recent events and your current physical condition it seemed logical to me that who ever had orchestrated this bizarre situation in the first place, was obviously playing us like a couple of puppets on strings. I mean, let's face it, it is not every day that a twenty million dollar work of art is stolen, let alone in such bizarre circumstances either, and removed under some very odd conditions that could be deemed beyond the normal run of things.

It also seems logical to assume that we might be getting set up by some international arts thieves or some unscrupulous antique dealers, or even a gang of very clever illusionists. But, either way we had better keep our wits about us. But, I don't mean that your tattoo is part of it, that in itself is an incredible occurrence, but for the image to be the same face on the oil painting as the Rossetti, well, for me that's far too coincidental.

I am afraid I cannot even begin to provide an answer or a rational explanation for the removal of the Hellfire Sword either, well not yet, anyway. But, in reality you would expect such a masterpiece, if stolen, to be found in a dustbin or discovered in some back street antiques' fair or something.

It would not be the first time a priceless antique has been discovered in a sale, now would it? We should check eBay, or visit a local car boot sale to see if it is lurking about there," he said flippantly, and stared back out of the passenger window in desperation as his mind juggled with the information, and jostled it around in his one and only complex little brain cell. "And, I also think this is not the last we have heard of this subject if you ask me.

But nice car, Darlene. I do like the high up observation position, you get a good view. And, you can see over the bushes into the greenery. I will tell you what has occurred though, Darlene, just recently I have had some very weird telephone calls. Tell me, have you received any odd letters or demands in the post recently?

Or ad hoc telephone calls where no-one has actually spoke on the phone, but just seemed to listen until you place the receiver back down, you know like a crank caller trying to piss you off? Or have you met with any weird or wonderful strangers? People who have asked for assistance in some strange way?

What I mean is someone who has suddenly popped up out of the blue and is trying to get back into your life for some reason? You should let me know, as it could be important, I have had some strange things happen, you know like every kind of day stuff, but they seem to be just more frequent."

Darlene flicked her hair backwards, thought for a bit, then responded, "As far as any strange and very odd people are concerned, there is only one I can immediately think of, and that is you, only you, Kemp Hastings, only you.'

Darlene turned and smirked, as Hastings smirked back at her and then smiled.

"Nope, just the electricity bill," she answered, then nodded in bemusement, as he shrugged his broad shoulders.

He spoke again, "Just the painting then, and a love letter from those greedy arsed electricity moguls who are just as bloody threatening with their demands for extortionate bills, just as terrorists are, if you ask me. But, then again, can't make tea without electrickery now can you? Those buggers know that very well. So, safe to assume that you have received no red letter mail offers or death threats or applications to join pyramid schemes on offer then? Well, that's a good start," he said, whilst shaking his head.

"None!" she replied. "I do, however, have Dante's twenty million dollar painting with me in the back of the car. Does that count? Thought I would bring it along and show you it, before I did anything stupid with it."

Hastings pointed forward and jerked his finger ahead. "Best not look at it here, we might crash another car."

Darlene agreed and drove the Range Rover a little bit faster towards the village of Farnell, just a few miles away from the Restenneth Priory—albeit heading in the opposite direction where the figure had recently appeared.

"You shouldn't drive for a couple of days you know. We will come back and pick up your beloved little car later, or you could contact a car recovery company, best leave it to the professionals."

She took another glance at the investigator, and thought that he had probably drifted off to somewhere in dream land as he normally did when caught in deep thought. She drove on.

"So tell me, what are you thinking about at this very moment in time, Kemp? You look a bit lost," she asked, wiping a few strands of red hair from her eye line again.

He slid his head off the window then straightened himself up, sniffed a little, then faced his companion. "Not sure, Darlene. I have an odd feeling that this biblical thing is not quite over yet. You see when we left the cemetery

The Silent Apostle II

in Dundee, I was 100% absolutely sure that things would just ease off and that your tattoo would simply disappear as with the Sadarium or Veronica's veil, you know after the period of lent, but apparently this is not the case.

I am still researching the subject, and may have to travel to Egypt for more answers. I have a friend in Cairo who has deep knowledge of the bizarre events in biblical history. He is of course a complete and utter pointy headed lunatic, but an amazing source of information. Do you fancy a trip to Cairo?" he asked.

Later that evening and in the quietness of his surroundings, Hastings picked up his little black book and quizzed its contents. Darlene, meanwhile, had made arrangements and was making her way back to the city.

He read the words he had written in his book whilst consuming a few healthy drams of brandy and slowly but surely drifted into a hazy state of happiness.

Rossetti.

Dante Gabriel Rossetti, born London 12th May 1828 and died of 'Bright's disease', 9th April 1882 Kent, London. Rossetti was an active member of the Pre-Raphaelite Brotherhood who changed the course of painting during the Victorian Era of British history.

Dante had painted 'The Damsel of the Holy Grail' in the year 1874 which depicts Mary Magdalene holding the Eucharistic chalice and is overseen by a bird of peace or a white dove.

> *Mary Magdalene or 'The Apostle's Apostle' travelled with Jesus to Jerusalem and was present at the crucifixion. Luke 8:3. Holy Bible. Mary Magdalene had taken the time to write a gnostic gospel of which many fragments have been found scattered across various countries. Several parchments have come to light dating in and around the 5th century.*

Just then, he was alerted by the sound of a loud bang. He jumped up, as the book he was holding fell from his grasp. He had momentarily fallen asleep and shuddered as he found his empty glass.

"Ah refill time," he said, then scrambled to his feet, just as a warm wisp of fresh air drifted through the room. Picking up his glass from the table, he negotiated his way back to the drinks' cabinet and stood staring at himself in the long ornate mirror whilst pouring himself another larger than normal size dram of brandy.

As he turned back toward the mirror, he stared at his image more intently and was almost amused to find it was not his reflection staring back at him. The drink had obviously taken the right effect he thought, then smiled at himself or whoever it was looking back.

"Who the bloody' hell are you?" he asked, as the reflection just stared back at him with no indication or signs of life or emotion. Hastings drifted more into a challenging prose. "Ah! Ah! Wait a moment—do not tell me? I know you. I have seen your sad and lonely face just recently, I know who you are! You are whatshisface, the poet, no that sculptor fellow, no the writer. No, oops, shhhh!" he slurred, whilst placing a single finger over his lips. "Don't tell me. I got it, you are that Rossetti, you are Gabdramelli Dante Rosmetti" He spluttered in his drunken verbal attack of the artist.

"You are a jack of all the artistic trades, them all, the painter, the soldier, the sailor but more importantly, le poet and le artiste . . . is that not correct?" he said, in his drunken stupor whilst still pointing at the reflection as the image shuffled its position and was moving closer towards the mirror as if to get a clearer view. Then the image smiled and nodded as if to acknowledge his remarks.

Hastings had a huge grin on his face as he recognised the artist who was now fully dominating his reflective life.

"So you are responsible for all this shit, are you? Do you know you are putting me through a living hell, and not just me either, but, me and my gal Dashlene, you and your vile laudanum opium sprees along with your acts of acute drunken-ness, your so called active involvement in unearthly pursuits of the black magic. Your high and mighty Victorian shodding values. I can't say I am that impressed, by your antics.

Well, can't say I blame you for actually for getting pissed, but dabbling in the Majick, well, that was bloody stupid, on your part, and your talents as an artiste, damn amazing, absolutely genius, if you ask me. But tell me why all the fuss? What is this shit all about? Why has Darlene been cursed? You tell me that, Mister El Dante," he asked, in his slurred speech attack on Rossetti, and then lifted his drink and saluted the figure in the mirror, as it appeared to gaze back at him.

Then the image spoke. "I am, as you say, Dante Gabriel Rossetti. Yes, I did dabble in hallucinogenic drugs and yes I do obey the darker side of the occult, and all to my sad demise, depending on your outlook of life and death. But you, Mister Kemp Hastings, well, you are a lot closer to me than you will ever actually know. Your friend, the beautiful Miss Gammay, she has crossed over, she has seen the other side of death, and has been blessed with hindsight and will take time to understand her role as she moves into our glorious ethereal world. She has been chosen by the Magdalena herself."

The image seemed to glow a bright blue as a haze of mist bellowed up from the bottom of its feet. Then the image stabilised as it spoke again, "Your time will come soon but please tell me one thing: what year is it?"

Hastings leaned closer to the mirror and gazed at the dress sense of the reflective image as Rossetti then took a single step backwards for a better view. Then he looked at his watch, it said the 12th May. Then he answered the great Rossetti's question. "It is the 12th of May in the year 2011 in the 21st century. What year did you think it was?"

No answer came as Hastings quizzed the image which was clad in its 18th century, heavy grey trousers and black waistcoat and tunic. The distinguished look of a man of substance, a man with influence and flair, especially on the day that marked his earthly death.

He spied the golden chain that linked the golden time piece attached to its end link, which was clipped to another heavy-linked gold chain running from the middle button hole of Rossetti's waistcoat where the watch itself sat snuggly in in the left side waistcoat pocket. The image was very much how Hastings had remembered what Dante Rossetti looked like on the picture that was neatly tucked into his little black book, along with his footnotes.

Rossetti looked much younger than his photograph depicted. His hair was more well-kept, receding a little but he was never-the-less a good looking man verging on the more mature side of life. He was clean and well-groomed.

The image was holding a black hat and was swaying from side to side, as it spoke softly to the investigator. "I have not died yet; none of us here on this dark plane have died. We live within the ether gases; we move as ghost-like figures and we have rational thoughts and urges, but, we have a balance to maintain, and you have a duty to perform."

Hastings took another drink of his beverage, then he mumbled a few words. "Well, if that is the case, then my duty is to my friends. But tell me Gab, I can call you Gab—yes, no? Doesn't really matter. But please tell me one thing, your Damsel of the Sank Real, is she real? Does that painting really capture her true likeness, and why would you want to inflict such an image on a living person?"

The image moved closer to the mirror as Hastings continued in his ramblings. Hastings heard echoes coming from his bathroom. It was a soft voice and it was very clear.

"This image is real and the events in your life are as real as you want them to be. She is the ultimate earthly entity; she can move in and out of reality just as she wishes. But she must also ensure that faith is maintained. The control of billions of 'souls' is important and much is at stake if we get it wrong."

Hastings was nodding abruptly as the strong alcohol was making a more potent and direct hit on his logical senses as he quizzed the entity further. "So, Gabriel, what do you want me to do? Because you and your ethereal friends have virtually thrown my life into turmoil and have ruined Darlene's life completely—what sort of bloody balance is that?"

The image placed the black hat on his balding head and removed the time piece from his waistcoat pocket, then began tapping the face of the watch. Hastings noticed that his lips did not move but the words were clearly heard.

"Look at the painting, Mister Hastings, observe the symbols and absorb the hidden esoterical messages captured within its framework. Read the maths and more importantly think about the woman in question, not the subject matter but the earthly woman. And, if you get time, come visit my graveside and ready my epitaph. We can talk there."

The mirror appeared to have glazed over and resembled what Kemp would describe as a cold front as the icy image started to disappear from view. Hastings hiccupped three times then burped and started waving goodbye to the mirror.

"Nice meeting you too, Mishter Gabriel, please do call again, but try using the damn door next time," muttered Hastings as he stumbled over the small table that lay in his way, missing the mirror by a few inches as he toppled over in a fit of laughter, then started laughing out loud as he grappled with his drunken state.

Then he was confused as he stared at the base of the mirror. He then reached out and grabbed the black hat that sat adjacent to the lion's claw and ball foot of the mirror stand.

"Thanks." Then he fell asleep on the floor.

Chapter Two
Epitaph

The following day Darlene and Kemp had met for lunch and were discussing all the facts that they thought they knew about mythology, folklore and history and then spent the complete day together. Yet Hastings had consciously failed to discuss the previous night's events in his drunken stupor let alone try and explain the advent of the mysterious bowler hat with her.

That same evening after an eventless sort of day, the two spent a good few hours discussing the way ahead with their predicament, Kemp could not simply understand how Darlene remained so nonchalant about recent events and was desperately struggling to make sense of something that was simply not rational to his logical mind.

Darlene, had remained overnight in Kemp's bachelor pad, love nest—the two having slept apart for the second time in their somewhat short liaison time frame. Yet they both would both agree a mutual respect for one another, but neither would rule out a bit of 'slap and tickle'.

And, although Kemp liked her a great deal, he didn't want to make any stupid 'amour' advances until he was absolutely certain that Darlene would reciprocate accordingly without leaving him sprawled across his Egyptian rug with his 'family jewels' wrapped around his throat.

Conversely, Darlene would be the first to admit that Hastings was too much like her father and even possessed the same body scent as he did. Her dad had sadly died some eight years earlier from a long illness. He had passed away just as she entered the university as a senior lecturer, but she would swear he was always around her, which often left her thinking if Kemp was related to her and she knew that she sniffed the odour around him far too much.

She would also admit that Kemp had the exact same mannerisms that her dad had possessed, and he even complained about the same things, which again, she found amusing but found herself all too often sitting back in admiration as Hastings explained almost any subject to her. Although there was a strange mental and physical attraction to him.

If Darlene was asked about Kemp Hastings being in her life, she would say that their relationship, for the time being, would be a very platonic one, as they would often sit and discuss the world's problems at great lengths to the wee small hours.

The morning came quick, albeit that Kemp had spent a fairly comfortable night on his large sofa with his aches and pains from his recent road accident, which had miraculously gone—apart from a slight stiffness around his shoulder muscles.

Darlene, on the other hand, had fallen into unconsciousness in the warm duvet of 'Kemp Hastings' land', for the second time and fuelled with a tot or two of brandy, and awoke to the morning chorus of the local rooster, nicknamed Lynford, as he informed the world that he was awake and still very alive much to the dismay of the village's inhabitants.

The name Lynford having been attributed to this huge, male chicken mainly because all attempts by its owner to catch the avian often resulted in the bird's owner coming second in the race of capture, and he had, on occasion, spent hours trying to catch the bird. Kemp had always thought he would get the feathery bastard with the Jag one morning, but the birdie was far too clever for mere humans.

Kemp had just flicked the 'on' switch to the kettle and was about to find the bread for toasting, when there was a loud knock on the downstairs entrance door. He flinched at first and thought that it might be the police checking up on him for leaving the scene of the previous day's accident. He quizzed the clock: it was nearly 08:15 hours.

He then made his way slowly downstairs and opened the door, gingerly at first, but to his delight there was no blue-uniformed officer to confront him, but he was presented with a stockily-built workman, who was instead clad in grey work overalls covered in a coating of light brown dust.

"Morning guvnor, what a nice day for it . . ." said the young man.

'Mr Hastings is it, can you sign here please?

Kemp nodded his head as he stood within the wooden doorway.

"Delivery for you. Where do you want it left?" asked the delivery man. "It's quite a large item, I can't bring it into the building it's over 25 kg, not allowed to lift that kinda shit, not these days with all that health and safety stuff going on.'

Kemp motioned the man to leave the package by the outside foyer or near to the gateway and said that he would pick it up later. The grey clad man just smiled and agreed, and after a short argument with the electronic signature pad, he wandered off back to his truck.

Kemp returned upstairs and grabbed the kettle, just as Darlene passed by the doorway, and was heading for the shower cubicle, muttering something in the realms of, "Coffee, really black and lots of sugar—I feel like shit." Then she disappeared off into the bathroom.

The delivery man, meanwhile, fired up the winch on the back of his IVECO flat bed truck and clipped on the hook to the lifting bridle. Then, operating the many control levers, he carefully lifted the slab slowly off his truck, then swung the granite plinth toward the grass verge and laid it neatly in the upright position against the larger of the two stone gate pillars.

The stone slab from what could be observed was clearly an old grave stone and was now somehow the new possession of Kemp Hastings of the Royal Order. It was then that he took another quick look out of the window having been alerted by the loud noise of the hydraulics of the winch truck. And he stood motionless as he watched the slab being placed in situ.

"What the hell is it this time?" He smirked and tutted, then returned back to his coffee, just as Darlene emerged from the shower all wrapped up snuggly in a Kemp Hastings' white, fluffy house coat and stood by the doorway.

"Anything interesting?" she asked, whilst grabbing the mug and began to take a sip of the hot, milky brew. Kemp, meanwhile, raised an eye brow and his left hand, then pointed somewhere towards the top of the window in a non-committed type of fashion, as if blaming the Gods for yet another act of ludicrous intervention.

"Nope, just another weird twist to this bloody crazy conundrum. I think this time someone has decided to send me a half ton grave stone, that's all, nothing normal."

Darlene almost froze in her tracks and smiled, then muttered. "Okay, then why on God's earth would you want to buy or acquire a grave stone, Kemp?" she asked, inquisitively then waited for an answer.

Kemp stood and stared at the plinth as it leant it up against the gate post, then he started shaking his head and turned to face her and then responded to the question. "Oh no, Darlene, not purchased, just bloody delivered. I think I may need to find it a new home or donate it to some church somewhere, who knows? Whatever bloody next?"

He then walked across the room to his modest library and extracted a clutch of documents from the middle shelf. His library mainly consisting of a multi-mixed compendium of spiritual, biblical and science fiction books. He had found himself returning to the same reference book time and time again, only this time he actually knew what he was looking for.

He picked up one of his older looking booklets and blew the light coating of dust away from the cover. The lettering appeared much clearer.

It read: **Incunabula**, version one—'Writ of Souls'.

He flicked through a few pages, then stopped and found an insert referring to the use of biblical weapons and methodology of the 5th century. He skipped the first few pages covering the Ark of the Covenant and the Art of Crucifixion, then he flicked between the Hellfire Cross Sword and the Spear of Destiny pages.

According to his manuscript the two items, the spear and the sword, were once combined together to bring the lands of the pharaohs together in unity. It was a strategic attempt to meld the upper and lower regions of Egypt together. This particular article of faith was to be the Pharaohs' ultimate 'weapon of choice' to control the Gods.

He had also been alerted to the existence of a single weapon that was used to send kings, gods, queens, sorcerers, sirens and beasts back into the underworld of Hades. It was rumoured that this 'spear tipped' sword could keep the Grim Reaper at sword's length and that was obviously a good thing.

Hastings had by default read Homer's 'Iliad': a paperback copy of which had conveniently come into his possession the previous year. He recalled the tail of Persephone and how desperate she was for revenge, tricking Odysseus and his crew into remaining on the mystical island.

A deceptive ploy in order to feed her not-so-endearing children, who were in fact a clutch of darling little demons.

Thinking about the demons aspect, instantly brought him back to Hades, and the Hellfire Sword itself.

A few pages further through the book and he found what he was looking for. He had read the passage several times before, but now, it had more significance.

"What a deception plan, good job the Greeks had their wits about them."

He ran his index finger down the page and stopped at page 137 and searched for paragraph 33 and took a deep breath before reading the text out loud as he began moving around his living quarters.

The page read: The Sword Hilt Manuscript

> *The God killing sword or the 'tartarus inferni' (Hellfire Sword), the haft or hilt is constructed from skin and bone and encased in a shroud of gold. The length of which will extend one arm's length plus one hand span of the intended user.*
>
> *The weight of which, is counterbalanced with a marble or glass pommel, the weight may shift from user to user. The blade will have been folded six times and overlapped seven times; the quillon will be attached and annealed.*
>
> *The thigh bone of the 'one' is the omnipotent source of power and thus carved into the haft of the Hellfire and shall be encased in gold and silver.*

> *The 'tartarus inferni' once constructed was rumoured to have been placed in the fires of eternity to enhance it with hidden properties. Its hardness and strength can only be matched with construction methods that only the sciences and techniques of the future will detect.*
>
> *The Haft is of hollow construction, and within it is lined with glass. It once contained a single page of hidden esoteric knowledge hidden in a crystal phial, placed in the void by physical intervention. Then the pommel is turned twelve times in an anti-clockwise direction to the lock position and further annealed.*
>
> *The quillon is made of the purest of gold and cross plated with diamond studs of six. The seamless work will be quenched in the blood of an ox and offered to the 'worthy' of the human society.*
>
> *End of text.   Signed, the Cipher.*

"Well if that is not modern day Apocrypha then I have no idea what the hell will be. Hey, listen to this, Darlene, this really has some heavy duty esoterical meanings."

Darlene gazed on with a slight bewildered look upon her face. Then challenged his comments. "Kemp, c'mon 'Apocrypha'? In what context do you mean? Secret religious meanings, writings and all that other stuff that never actually made it into the humble bible—that kind of Apocrypha? Now that will be interesting to hear about."

She tilted her head then finished drinking her beverage whilst staring at the investigator. Hastings shuffled his feet as he read further through the book and began wandering about his flat like a motivated biblical professor—an unconscious habit that he did at times like this.

Frequently, he would stop reading the text and look back at Darlene as if he was searching for clarity or deeper understanding. She sat and watched with great interest.

"Is there any other kind? Well, in this context anyway. I mean this is the 21st century, after all, and we have all seen the X-files on the television. For me, well, I still have an inclination of perhaps a pre-human existence on our little planet, or at least an ancient alien relationship that maybe has died away, out of existence through time. If you want to get bi-polar regarding academics and fact.

So, what I think is that we have here is a 'metaphor' of power and control, because I do happen to know that Apocrypha in the Greek language, as an example, basically means, 'those hidden away', and that must mean people or a life form.

You know if we say 'those cups are hidden away', that would not make exact sense, but from an academic standing would you agree the term life form? Defined in this case by the word 'those' or let us just suppose for one moment that we are actually talking extra-terrestrial life forms, and that's where I become very, very uneasy and uncomfortable."

Darlene was nodding her head and had been slowly tapping the side of the porcelain mug, using the gold ring as a percussion tool in time with the music in the background.

She shifted her position and pulled her legs up under her buttocks, then leaned over the back of the soft sofa and followed Hastings around the room with her eyes as he narrated verbatim from the informative book.

"Again all dubious wording and could be utter garbage in all their content. But I also understand that Judaism as a further example of Apocrypha, and that could be the ultimate message that is captured within the Dead Sea Scrolls.

But, the problem here is word of mouth, or Chinese whispers as the message through the passage of time has been added with arms and legs and stories of simple, things like ancient warring skirmishes over time became great, unprecedented wartime events, and all due to poetic verbal licence.

So what do I have? Not a damn lot. I can only imagine that something more corroborative will pop up?" He turned and smiled as he watched his house guest drape herself over the back of his soft Mexican sofa.

"Ok, Mister Hastings, your secret codes, all this secret information passed through time . . . Are you saying that the Bible is just a big code book? Or are you saying that only specific portions of the Apocrypha or some detailed, esoteric literature was recorded in the Bible and that there is actually another copy of the Holy Bible somewhere? a physical book packed with hidden knowledge.

Because, if that is the case, then, you should not dismiss the complete Gnostic gospels of the Saints or the Nag Hammadi Scrolls either, as they are also littered with your apostle's verbal outpourings and maybe even be riddled with fable type conjecture and yet, Kemp, one point six billion Catholics globally hinge their beliefs upon these ideals and more so upon these very documents.

The Silent Apostle II

So the esoteric and the apocryphic messages could be 'the real' message from God, purely because the way they have not only survived man handling, but evolved through the centuries, and have made their way into modern day existence, and that process in itself is very secret, or was controlled with acute precision by a much higher Order in society."

Hastings was nodding his head again, and rubbed the pages with his left hand. "Doctor Gammay, I totally agree, so here is the million dollar question: How many damned aliens are amongst us today, or let us be even clearer: How many Angels of Death or Angels of Mercy co-exist within the complex fabric of our mixed society? All scarey stuff. But, let me change the subject just for one second, listen to the radio right now, this very second, can you hear that Boney M record?"

Hastings pointed to his iPad that was playing softly in the background—the sound track of early 80's and 90's music was quietly humming away as the couple conversed. Darlene was still tapping away on her mug with her ring to the very tune.

"Well, you will just love this bit: now think 'out of the box' and think about 'ancient psalms'—what if I said that Psalm 137 was behind the very message that this record alludes to? Sounds quite silly unless you actually know or understand history. And of course, my dear Doctor, you do," he said, pointing his index finger straight at his colleague.

"By the rivers of Babylon, we sat and wept, blah, blah, blah. I am sure you have heard it a zillion times. But what does it actually refer to? Not just the psalm itself, but the psalm number 137 itself. And again, this is another example of an esoteric reference or meaning. A number that can be found in many disciplines of either mathematics, religion, physics and more.

But since we are discussing religion, let's go to Babylon, or Iraq. Zion . . . the Bible gateway to the new world; a place of heaven on Earth. Well, I would certainly challenge that concept today, but it is both an amazing place and an interesting number nevertheless—if you wish to delve that far into the subject.

So, let us suppose that you could interpret it and say it refers to a date—1st March 2007-1007 or AD 7 BC 7, or conversely, 1/3/7. But, it is indeed the 33rd prime number in a given sequence. Or, if we go a bit deeper a Chen Prime. And that is not common in any equation.

Conversely, Darlene, in physics, it could be interpreted as a fine structure content or the number could be broken down to the 'nth' degree and even relate to an integer number, but that is all far too complex for my little brain to work out.

So, I opt for the more esoteric angle, the age of the universe, or its given age when it was first recorded, and could be roughly relative to an example such as '137' (x) times the square of a myriad of years, or cubed to a specific mass of an interstellar planet or heavenly body, a star—pick one, Darlene, there are literally millions to choose from?

Let us say Mintaka, within Orion's belt, how could we ever work out its mass and density? Well, esoterics and geophysical tellurics and all that kind of stuff all hang on the 137 numerical notion of mass, and I have no idea where that number actually comes from.

So the other question is: why do I think this is the better option? I hear you cry. Well, my dear lady, it is simply because it will never be proven or disproven. And again, if I was to ask 'why bother to record such detail in the first place?' Especially if it was not relevant, but why record on such important religious documents or scriptures?

My theory would aim toward space travel, all far-fetched stuff but someone thought it important enough to inform future mankind of a simple set of numbers." He pursed his lips and took a very deep breath. "I think I am at the end of my intellectual capacity to work this sword conundrum to any solid conclusion yet."

He then walked out of the room, heading for the kitchen humming the tune 'By the Rivers of Babylon', with his book of hidden knowledge, 'The Incunabula', flapping loosely about in his hand.

Darlene shuffled in the sofa and spoke out loud, in order to catch his ear. "Kemp, you are aware that the Aramaic version of Psalm 137 relates to the daughter of Babel, aren't you, or the heavenly destroyer, and, if you are looking for a metaphor then goodness there is the best one right there.

But the foreign land reference is also clear, but that just means to me that the song of the Lord will hail from another country, having had Babel destroyed. Oh! That is creepy, you know we have just had the Gulf war. And if we were to get esoterical then we would also have to seek out Nostradamus and see what else he had to say five hundred years back, let alone what these writings tell us from as far back as biblical times."

Hastings returned to the room and passed her a big chocolate éclair.

"Okay what's that for?" she asked, abruptly.

Kemp Hastings stood upright and stared at her for several seconds. "To eat, my dear lady, what do you want to do with it?" he said, flippantly, then laughed.

"So, Aramaic the old world biblical language and Psalm 137 answers all our questions, does it? Nice chocolate—don't you think? Very creamy, mmh, think I will have another one," he said, then wiped the cream away from his lower lip. "It takes away the pain of that bloody car crash; I still get little twinges now and again. But you might be right with the Aramaic stuff, we will have to look a bit deeper, not sure how the sword and the psalm relates together but interesting nonetheless."

Hastings sat next to Darlene and opened his laptop.

"Here look I think I have found something, I am in the book of Genesis and it mentions the daughter of Zidon. Well, that's the place, Zion, and the location of Tyre. Now, is that the Tyre, as in William of Tyre, regarding the Knights' Templars and all that, or is it another place entirely?

I don't know as yet. This psalm 137 and all its contents refers to 'affections or disagreements' with the truth, basically explaining arguments against what is in place, so, in this case the daughter's references here, are classed as indications or notions.

Well, that does not help us but it does show us that people were giving early warning to what was transpiring. Nope, sadly that's a dead end, but it shows you that a simple bit of music can be riddled with hidden meanings and that is how esoterics works. Anyway, this Incunabula book has answered my questions. All we need to do is find out where the sword is located and we are in good shape."

The Silent Apostle II

The Doctor wiped her lips with her tissue leaving a small blob of chocolate éclair on her check. Hastings leaned forward as Darlene closed her eyes. "Messy pup, that you are, one dark chocolate éclair and look at the state of you, choccy drops everywhere." He wiped her cheek then closed the lid of the computer.

Chapter Three
A brush with the law

Later that morning, Darlene had returned to her flat, and spent a couple of hours answering emails and paying her bills online, a certain chore, like most working people, she hated doing, but it was a necessary evil to exist in the modern world.

After a relaxing few hours, she drifted off into a hazy kind of sleep, never really quite getting comfortable and tossed and turned as her mind was playing catch-up with the current events.

She then heard what she thought was a loud bang, and was rudely awoken from her semi-slumbered state. She quizzed the clock; it said twenty past seven. She had been asleep for an hour, or so she had thought.

After taking a few moments to fully wake herself up, she worked out that she had been sleeping for a good ten hours, with yet another strange dream for her to work out.

Her dream recurred in her thoughts—the words in the newspaper headline had said:

>'Doctor Darlene Gammay receives finder's fee for stolen Rossetti!'

There was a sudden commotion outside in the narrow street; it was created by the animosity of the local constabulary, as a big, white 4 x 4 police car came to a screeching halt with its blue lights flashing followed by a series of bursts from the multi-tone air horns. The noise of the high pitched sirens making their unwelcomed presence known, not only in the street but probably half of the city.

Outside her apartment's entrance doorway, three policemen stood in anticipation, awaiting orders from their HQ. The radio had buzzed a couple of times then the words 'Go, go, go' echoed in the small hallway.

Another police Range Rover pulled up very slowly in almost silence and headed towards number thirty three, then came to a halt a few yards from the doorway, which was followed by another bout of screaming and shouting orchestrated by police command as mayhem ensued.

Two officers armed with long steel fence posts were running headlong towards the house with their heavy steel post battering rams ready for deployment in order to break down the next difficult door.

Darlene panicked slightly, and hid the masterpiece neatly under her bed—the blue tube clearly sticking out at one end. She slowly moved the curtain to one side and took another peak outside. It was just then that her doorbell rang, she jumped and flinched momentarily catching her breath. She fluffed her hair up and pulled her cardigan down over her bosom, then took several deep breaths.

Walking very slowly towards the door, she took a glance backwards thinking that this could be her last day of freedom having been convicted of receiving stolen goods. Then she placed the security chain across door lock, and opened the door to the limit of the brass chain.

The chain links chinked somewhat apathetically as the door creaked as it came to a stop, and when a quarter open, she peeped gingerly out.

"Morning miss, can I have your signature please?" came the sharp voice of a deliveryman. "I have a registered letter for you."

Darlene had been half expecting to meet the dark figures of the local constabulary and was slightly confused and yet very relieved as she grabbed the electronic signature pad from the delivery man as he slid it between the door and the door frame.

She looked up, smiled, then scribbled her name across the small screen. She paused and shook her head, then quizzed the UPS delivery man's attire, acknowledging his big red ID Badge, and the bright green uniform.

She noticed the letters UPS on the upper left pocket then waited for a few seconds more and unlatched the chain and opened the door and returned the electronic device to its owner.

The delivery man handed over the envelope, then spoke. "Looks like number 27 are being raided for drugs, Miss, noisy buggers the police. Did you know that just last week they raided my neighbour's house, and it was the wrong address, completely trashed the front door. They said that the police and the security people are reading all our emails these days—no escape from big brother—slimy buggers," he said, then tipped his hat and made off down the stairway.

Darlene looked out of her door, she glanced to her left and watched as the inhabitants of number 27 were being dragged unceremoniously and thrown into a big, white waiting police van. She estimated that there were at least fifteen officers for two arrests.

"Morons!" she whispered, then she closed the door to her apartment.

She looked carefully at the envelope, and noticed it had various odd postal markings with five international franking stamps from as far away as Malta and Egypt in the top right corner, and another series of franking machine marks that read 'Artefacts and Paintings'—The Gallery, London.

She returned to her living room and threw the envelope on the sofa. She had definitely suffered enough surprises for the time being and she wandered off into her kitchen.

Chapter Four
Cairo

Noun—'Assignation' a clandestine meeting or tryst

Cairo was becoming blistering hot, even at seven o'clock in the morning of late August and the dusty city streets were bustling with a hive of activity; the traffic was chaotic and the local inhabitants were busy beavering away in their daily routines, or travelling to and from work.

The hum of twenty million people waking up in modern day Cairo was not a quiet affair by any standards. Hastings had already been disturbed by the 5.25am religious calling, having been blessed with a huge mosque with at least forty loudspeakers attached to it, which was located near to the hotel. It was the daily reminder in order to alert the Muslim world that it was time for prayer; luckily for him it was right opposite his hotel window.

"Ahh, Cairo, what a pain in the arse, what a good morning wake up call, glad I do not live here," he muttered, and headed for the shower knowing full well that the water was going to be cold—it was just an expectation and a fact of life he had become accustomed to whilst visiting the land of the chicken kebab.

The holy ritual of Ramadan had just passed and Eid had recently finished; the many street vendors were out and about touting for new business and the many tourists were being consistently accosted and bombarded by street urchins and the many stall or shop owners who were open for new business.

Two hours later, Kemp Hastings smiled as the taxi driver pulled up against the overly sized pavement and came to a halt. As he opened the door and stepped out, he was hit by the inner city pungent smell and aroma of the over populated Cairo air. Just as the warm humidity wrapped itself around his olfactory nasal senses, he almost choked and sneezed twice.

He threw his black 'North Face' rucksack over his left shoulder sending a shower of warm, wet sweat up his back. As he turned to walk away from the cab, there was another 'toot' from an adjacent car's horn, it was another taxi, and the driver had begun waving his arms.

Kemp laughed, momentarily reminiscing about the almost laughable taxi driver culture in Egypt: the driver's would often watch you arrive at your stop, then as you stepped out from your current taxi you would hear the words "Taxi, Meester?"

Laughing out loud, he closed the door of the car and walked towards the huge gates of the Museum, only pausing for a few seconds to take in the amount of devastation that the old parliament building had suffered, along with the disrupted locality of Tahrir Square. Darlene meanwhile had headed off on an earlier shopping spree with one of her friends, as she probably knew Cairo better than Kemp ever could.

Hastings watched intently as the military arm of the country's dishevelled government assembled itself across what remained of the old inner city square. Each soldier was standing upright to attention, armed with a baton and a shield whilst standing shoulder to shoulder and rubbing up against their counterparts. The troop began deploying in a huge, circular formation.

He watched with interest as the young Officers inspected the troops one by one, only stopping now and again to adjust a baton or reset a hat, here and there, yet their own attire was somehow just as ill fitting. Hastings smiled again and shook his head in amazement.

He quizzed the backdrop of the surrounding area, it was strangely dominated by a huge, singular building; the very structure which overshadowed the beautiful Cairo Museum itself, the now, dormant shell of what once appeared to be a rather substantial construction of dwellings and offices which had been destroyed by fire—a gutted derelict carcass and a stark reminder of change and reform.

The structure had been subject to an arson attack during the chaos that had ensued earlier in the year, and was completely burned out along with several other buildings. A reminder of what the lack of democracy and control could inflict on the local government if they could not keep the electorate happy.

It was now the month of September, and yet not so long ago back in January the square would have been impossible to visit as the revolution had sparked off and gripped Egypt in its violent struggle for democracy.

Kemp thought for a moment as to how the government could even try and gain control of 22 million people,

The Silent Apostle II

especially so many in one large city—yet so widely dispersed.

"Mmmh!" he smirked, then walked on.

During the short car journey from a local district known as Maadi, the taxi driver had explained that the government motorcade of the newly informal, unelected new government had left a secret location somewhere deep within Cairo's established inner city. And heading through the square en-route to the Egyptian embassy.

The car-cade or cortege then was due to travel onwards to the government offices. It was then that the driver turned the Blaupunkt radio off for one reason or another, and took a few short cuts up some unkempt side streets. The President, who still lay apparently in an induced drug-controlled sleep was in the worst kept secret location in Egypt, known as The Cairo General hospital, with an armed guard patiently waiting outside.

Pending his international court appearance, and was apparently not running the country and the elected committee had worked through as contingency under the new regime for revolutionary change over-shadowed by the Military.

The court case against him for his crimes against the Egyptian people and humanity was imminent, but the people were not happy with the armed services hovering in the political background. It was obvious that the people wanted the President out of the equation and the outcome of an 'in country trial' would most likely result in a very long term prison sentence or the death penalty for the outgoing tyrant.

Democracy was evidently beginning to take its iron fist grip on society as many local women had adopted to dress down for the occasion—each adorned with flip flops and cut down shorts. Hasting's instant thoughts were tourists, but no, he was wrong, these were indeed local girls and women.

He then slowly made his way to the museum's entrance and passed through the huge metal gates having paid his 60 LE, and was ascending the wide stairway into one of the world's greatest museums.

Several populated tiers of nothing but granite sarcophagi and huge door lintels that ran across the many wide doorways. Each chamber was adorned with a range of huge, glass cabinet display cases that littered the ground level where each display case must have weighed at least a metric ton each. 'Just adding to the hundreds of tons of existing masonry,' thought Hastings as he sniffed the scent of a vanilla aroma that filled the air.

In the office to the immediate left of the main entrance hallway, Dr Mohammed Elfeky was sitting quietly absorbing the local paper with his eyes closed. His brown-stained tea cup was resting precariously on the edge of the chair's wooden arm, potentially waiting to be knocked off its perch, and would undoubtedly end up falling and smashing on the stone floor at any second.

Kemp spied his friend then quietly made his way into the middle of the office and stared at the chaos in the small room: it was littered with everything but office equipment. He laughed inwardly laughed and raised his voice towards the sleeping Professor.

"No time for sleeping Elfeky you lazy rag headed bum, get your skinny Egyptian arse off that chair and make a proper cup of tea," barked Hastings, placing his black rucksack bag on the adjacent rickety wooden table top. Mohammed Elfecky suddenly stirred then slid off the chair, momentarily springing to attention just as the porcelain cup hit the floor and bounced twice towards the small statue of Seth that was sitting nearby.

The cup then flipped onto its base and ended up sitting snugly between the feet of the granite statue, the contents of which had spilled onto the stone floor.

Kemp stared for a few seconds and thought that the statue was totally misplaced in the corner of the office as opposed to being on display for Mr Joe Public.

"Wahid, wahid," (one, one) Elfecky shouted, spying the tall figure of Hastings towering over him.

Kemp wiped his own brow with his handkerchief, then addressed the not-so-sleeping Professor of Egyptian Archaeology and artefacts. "Do you still walk like an Egyptian then?" he muttered, offering him a friendly hand up.

"Salaam, salaam, oh what joys! Welcome to Cairo, Mister Hastings, good to see you again. How are you? It has been such a long time? How was your trip from Scotland? And, my apologies for dozing off, I have been working too many hours this week, a quick power nap does one's body clock good things you know. I expected you much later on today," he replied.

Kemp smiled and shook hands with Dr Elfecky. "So I see," he remarked, taking a seat and simultaneously opening up his bulging back pack.

"This is for your good lady hanum . . . (wife)," responded Hastings, passing a brown package across to the Egyptian. "I hope she likes strawberry jam?"

The Professor graciously accepted his gift.

"Ah, Meester Hastings, today it will be for my wives, for I am blessed with two," he said, proudly just as Hastings turned and stared into the eyes of Mohammed.

Then Hastings spoke as a teacher would to a child. "Ah well, there's the penalty and the problem right there Mohammed: two mother in laws to fight with, two witches from Hades to keep you in a reasonable order, oh what joys!" Then laughed out loud. "My colleague Dr Darlene will pop around later, she is off shopping somewhere, she was intent on buying some original oils for relaxation purposes. She said she will be about an hour or so. I am sure you will like her—she is your total opposite in character."

Kemp removed a piece of parchment from his satchel and passed it across the table to Mohammed who had just placed two cups of brown liquid that almost resembled tea on the table top.

Tea that would smell more like ginger or warm almonds than actual tea if Kemp had not known any better. He knew a bit about the many strange herbal teas and remedies that adorned the land of the Pharaohs and knew very well they had medicinal uses, let alone great for cleaning your intestines and insides.

"Your special tea, Mister Hastings," he said, dropping two sugars in the milky white cup.

"Thank you, Mohammed, another opportunity to chill out. Very glad you responded to my emails."

The Egyptian artefacts manager stood up then closed the door to the office and sat down again, then tapped the keyboard of his laptop.

"Yes, it was an unusual correspondence, quite cryptic, no idea what the hell you were asking for, though, but I knew you would venture out here at some point, Kemp, you normally do."

Hastings placed the satchel on the floor next to his seat and looked up, as the professor sat down in the rickety chair. Then the professor spoke, "What is this journey really about this time, Mr Kemp, more coins for selling, or are you searching for those little gold scarab things that you seem to adore, or is it the hidden obelisk of Khufu scenario?" he asked, then tapped his nose as if to acknowledge that all was to be discussed on the quiet.

Hastings scratched the back of his head then spoke. "In total honesty, I am not really sure Mohammed, but I am drawn here again by fate, and that much is for sure, maybe it's because I like the Egyptian sun, because it is certainly not the food, nor the bloody tea, but, it could be the chocolate and the dates though. But luckily for Egypt this is not a wild goose chase this time Mohammed, but a journey of real discovery, a trip with a real purpose, a journey of adventure and mystery that I just simply cannot explain, just yet. You see I have two subjects to get my head around." Hastings paused and tapped his leather satchel.

"I am actually looking for a chalice, the one that is depicted here on this manuscript, here, look, the cartouche is simple, but if you look at what the cartouche actually has written within it, well I am not sure what it actually means." He then pointed to the, now very interested, Egyptian a few symbols that had been written on the vellum.

Elfecky gazed over the document for approximately two minutes then spoke. "Oh, my goodness this is indeed an odd one, and a relatively new subject to me. But, this is not a copy of the holy chalice that you might think you may have in Europe, or conversely, the one that your scholarly lot seem to always go on about, this is quite unique, and something very different indeed, and equally as potent, if not more dangerous."

Kemp scratched his eye brows then asked a few more questions. "Do you know what it is? Or where it may be located then? And can I get my hands on it?" he asked, slurping the warm sample of murky Nile water, that was thinly disguised as herbal tea in the offering.

"Not me, I am afraid, Kemp, this is not my particular subject matter or my niche. But here in Cairo, I will, however, bet you that I know a man who can. Here look at this!"

Mohammed pulled at what appeared to be an old, dusty leather bound book that was stuck amongst some other journals. Kemp caught sight of the front cover as it emerged out from under the column of literature. It read: 'European religious cards' 1800's.

Professor Elfecky skipped a few pages, then stopped at a series of sketches based around drinking vessels and ran his index finger down the page.

"Now, let me tell you about all these chalices or cups, some of them in the past have been made into engravings, mostly copper or thin plate gold articles, and I do mean actually engraved onto a flat plate. I have seen one example hanging in the tomb of St somebody or other somewhere in my travels, but sadly, my memory fails me just at the moment. And, there is another example which is reported to be housed in the museum archive in the holy city of M'dina, Malta. I really can't remember exactly where, but somewhere near the old central Temple Cathedral museum. Have you ever been to Malta, Kemp?"

The investigator nodded his head in acknowledgement and pointed to the sketch book again and answered. "Not for some time, but I could do with a holiday though."

The professor continued in his search. "Now these elegant copper cups are said to be the vessels of the Magi, or the group of clerics who visited the infant Christ when he was born. There were three such chalices originally, but, one of them was destroyed by Caesar in one of his many angry outrages.

And it was rumoured that the chalice had been sliced into many tiny fragments, somewhere along the historical line, and the fragments were eventually gathered together and melted down. After the re-smelting, the cup was then cast or beat into a single thin plate of copper, and an image of which was a holy chalice was impressed upon the plate but interestingly enough it was rumoured that this receptacle was to possess strange chemical properties."

Kemp stroked his chin and smiled. "Your tea is really crap by the way. But go on, Mohammed, this is getting interesting." Hastings removed his hat and placed it on his knee. "What kind of strange properties, magnetic, fluorescent, three dimensional, what?" he asked.

Elfecky then rubbed his chin again then spoke. "'Well, this particular chalice when it is laid flat can be seen as a normal flat plate, but under certain lighting conditions it could be observed to take the form of a physical drinking vessel—a cup that can be used to store fluid. Magnetic it could be, which would explain how the cup could then be returned to its flattened state. Quite odd, don't you think?"

Hastings shrugged his shoulders and contemplated the Professor's explanation of the chalice. He knew that if Mohammed was aware of such things then there was a good chance that it was a true depiction or account regarding these artefacts.

Elfecky was a man with a certain charisma about him and he possessed a strange wealth of knowledge that often left you wondering when his brain was going to burst open. He knew just about anything or everything about Egyptian culture and folklore that was to be had, even more so in his field of study.

Academics world-wide would be humbled as to how one person could be so well-informed about everything. Kemp took the opportunity to pose another line of questioning toward the omniscient Mohammed. "Mohammed, what do you know of the Sanctos Epistula—Magdalena?" Then he waited patiently for an answer.

The Egyptian Professor pondered for a while and closed the book. He then took a very heavy, deep breath.

"Mister Hastings, you know in your field of Christian study that some things in life are just not meant to be touched, they should be left alone and not even discussed, but, my friend, you know this already, and this subject is probably most definitely one of them. Why do you choose to dabble in such things? I take it she, the 'Sanct Magdalena' our divine lady, has turned up again.

I assume no doubt appearing in some obscure mountain village in rural Mauritania or Brazil, or in a church or other place of worship, the same way she has just popped up through the centuries in order to have a look, and to say hello, to the modern world." He posed his synopsis, then left very little time for Hastings to answer.

"She, my friend, is the holiest of holy entities. She is a roaming free spirit, more of a manifestation than an actual solid visitation, normally turning up for a brief period of time then disappearing into obscurity. But, tell me, my friend, why do you ask?"

Kemp spent a few minutes explaining how Dr Darlene Gammay had suffered the blessings of the Magdalene

The Silent Apostle II

and her visitation; then after her appearance Darlene was inflicted by having a huge tattoo of her holy face emblazoned across her back and shoulder, appearing on her skin without any rational reason or explanation.

Well, that was apart from her being singled out for this curse in her own domestic bathroom, and not discounting the possibility that a visitor could have appeared from outer space and cast this imprint on her body as far as Darlene was concerned. But it was fact that someone's image was imprinted on her skin that frightened her most. An image that was delivered by no physical means and imprinted within a matter of eight hours duration as Darlene apparently slept.

The revelation of what is known as 'an illuminated manuscript' had somehow impacted or was indirectly related to the recent theft and removal of the mythical Tartarus Inferni Hellfire Sword.

The article was removed from what was deemed a very secure Vatican vault in Italy, and conversely, a Rossetti painting of the Magdalene had also been stolen from the national Italian art gallery in Roma.

As Hastings explained the amazing story, Doctor Elfecky appeared to be unmoved by the series of strange events being disclosed, it was as if he was half expectant of the outcomes.

Hastings further explained about the sword weighing almost six kilograms, that was observed vanishing from the Vatican and reappearing at the will of whoever or whatever was in control.

Recently, the sword had been moved across the globe from the Vatican to Scotland and then back again, somehow being transported as a solid object by what Kemp could only describe as a free forming floating vapour, orchestrated by a series of entities or ghostly visions which have the ability to physically move solid objects.

Kemp struggled to find the relationship between these events whilst at the same time contemplating why a twenty million dollar painting was removed also by mysterious means, and coincidentally of which resembled the tattoo on Darlene's body. His problem was finding a distinctive connection.

The Professor listened with great interest and nonchalantly drank his cup of Nile water as Kemp delivered the strange turn of events that had led him back into the land of the Pharaohs.

"Mohammed, this is not normal biblical stuff, this is quite scary, you know what I really think, I think that we are being manipulated by an unseen power."

Elfecky sniffed the warm air then spoke. "Unseen power? If you want to witness an unseen power, then you want to walk around this museum at night time, my friend, I will show you an unseen power, the guards here, will only work in pairs, and trust me they can tell you some stories that would make your lovely head of hair turn grey very quickly."

The two then discussed the matter further into the wee small hours.

Chapter Five
'The Disappearing Chalice'

After their heavy discussion, Hastings posed a few more questions. "So, do you think I could locate and purchase this chalice from your source Mohammed?" he asked, whilst scribbling some numbers and an address down in his little black note book. The cover of which was embossed with logo that depicted: *'HMSO'*

The Professor stood up and stretched his over indulged and non-athletic frame. "This is Egypt, my friend, the promised land, and the land of the ancient Pharaohs. You can purchase just about anything in this land if the price is right, and of course if you know who to talk to," explained the good Professor. "But first, let me make a few phone calls."

He then drank some of his off-coloured tea. Hastings, meanwhile, opened another book and quizzed its bland pages, then listened as Mohammed spoke. "So, she has emerged again has she? Popped up into the fabric of human existence. The last time she was around was over one hundred and fifty years ago. I think she was last seen somewhere in France. It was an appearance where some peasant girl claims to have conversed with her directly throughout the period of lent, and probably several weeks thereafter."

Hastings suddenly found the need to engage the Professor in the subject matter of Mary Magdalene in light of recent events, and shuffled his chair a little closer to perhaps the only man on the planet who could provide a rational explanation of events.

"So, Mohammed, since we are talking about the Apostles, what do you make of the advent of the Nag Hammadi scrolls and their revelations? In particular the lost gospel of Judas. Do you think there is any truth in these parchments from what you can deduce?" Hastings waited patiently as the Professor dropped a piece of lemon in his tea and started to stir it around with his pencil.

He took some time to consider the question before answering. "Mmmh, very interesting and very complicated question to ask, Kemp. You see we have several institutions and ideals at work here. Firstly, I know for a fact that the carbon 14 dating test on the Dead Sea Scrolls and some of the Nag Hammadi are consistent in their actual composition and have been dated precisely within less than a hundred years of Jesus's life on the planet.

The conundrum is, who actually wrote them in the first place, because the lost gospel scroll, well, the newly found gospel scroll of Escariot, was most likely written by a cleric with very opposing views to what was being actually communicated to the masses, regarding the role of Judas Escariot in the Bible.

Or conversely, and more along my lines of thought that they were written by a cleric who belonged to the family 'Escariot' and perhaps wanted to twist the biblical story toward making Judas out to be more of a devout disciple working under the premise of openly identifying Jesus's physical body to the Romans, and perhaps for specific purposes, which may have even been orchestrated by Jesus himself.

And, not to be seen as the traitor that he was depicted as, but nevertheless a man who still sealed his own fate by his negative actions. You see, Kemp, when you look at the actual text, it is very controversial, but it does not make it false in its content, it just provides an opposing account of events written by a credible source.

I am of the opinion, and this is my opinion only, Mister Hastings, that perhaps there was a secret pact by Jesus and Judas, a pact of mutual trust. I mean who really knows, as there were so many strange events occurring at that time. During this turbulent time there was such a flurry of activity that even the scribes themselves had difficulty keeping up with biblical facts and events."

Mohammed stopped talking for a few moments and was nodding his head as he gazed into the black residue in his cup. Kemp had an inclination that the Professor was an active Gnostic who knew a great deal about esoterics than he was letting on about.

He also knew that Egyptian Gnostics possessed a hidden or very secret understanding of the mystical side of the church as he had attended a closed conclave with some very strange people in St Paul's Cathedral in London not so long ago.

"You see, Kemp, if the church accepted the lost gospel of Judas, then they would as an institution would have to not only re-write biblical history, but change the way we view the positive and negative aspects of our religious beliefs in general, so the powers that be, deemed it a fake.

These Egyptian desert dwelling monks who preserved such detail, they refused to destroy the gospels in their possession. I mean this is the four main gospels of Matthew, Mark, Luke and John, maybe not written by them in their own hand, but a detailed account documented by their followers, you could interrogate the Qumran Essenes.

The gospels were seen as very antagonistic and the Bishop of Alexandria wanted them out of the way, he wanted them destroyed, as they added distraction to his master plan of keeping order in the church. Does that make any sense to you?" asked the Professor, whilst clasping his hands together.

Hastings leaned forward slightly in his chair, then offered a response. "Yes, it does make sense to me. But are you saying that for obvious control reasons they were left out or never referenced by those clerics who wanted their version of the Bible in the public domain, or the winners version of events."

The Professor was still nodding as he drank his lemon tea. Hastings smiled and continued. "So, let me tell you what I think, and I am no academic as you know Mohammed, but, in the year 1945 these so called lost gospels came to light after being discovered by a farmer near to Nag Hammadi, the discovery which led to a series of scrolls written by several of the Apostles or their followers at some point in their lifetimes.

I am personally more interested in the lost gospel of Mary Magdalene that was discovered in 1896, and other texts of this so called other Mary gospel, which also came to light as being written nearer to the 5th century.

And I understand that other portions of the texts had been dated to around the 2nd or 3rd century. I really do not know, but I would love to get my hands on them, and so would Darlene. I also understand that some of the detail verges on Gnostic mysticism and Jesus may have disclosed information to Mary that would take us away up into the heavens, and that's where my interest in heavenly bodies takes a whole new angle. Imagine for one minute that Mary Magdalene who was a serious inner circle contender, and who literally challenged all conventions relating to Christian belief in a man's world.

Maybe because she knew that there was another world that took the journey of the 'soul' through the Styx and into the realms of both angels and demons. If Mary was part of the GMSC or the 'Gnostics Mystical Select Circle' who were perhaps influential in every aspect of Bible culture, then we see another dimension completely.

The results which could lead to a journey to and from the afterlife. Now tell me, Mohammed, where does that put the church? But more so, does it confirm the belief of the ancient Pharaohs and their ascension to the stars, but the question is, who told the Pharaohs of this secret pathway to the stars?"

Elfecky responded. "Kemp, these episodes only last for a few of weeks, but who knows, I wasn't there, however, since we are talking about things that suddenly turn up, let me show you our new exciting exhibit—it's our new and very exciting sarcophagus."

The Professor was very uneasy as he sat facing Hastings; he too had an inclination that Hastings had obviously conducted some heavy duty research and was almost knocking on the door to the GMSC for clarity.

"Mister Hastings, I believe you may have to meet some people I know, they will perhaps bring a bit of greater clarity to your line of questioning. It is an amazing subject, Kemp, a world within a world, or a world out with a world, let's discuss this later."

Meanwhile, Kemp had stood up and leaned up against the statue of Seth, and drank his tea and watched as the Professor quizzed some paperwork then dragged him across to his new exhibit.

After about fifteen minutes, Mohammed's mobile phone danced across the sarcophagus top and buzzed a series of Arabic noises. Mohammed flipped the phone open and smiled as he read the text message. "Looks like you are in luck my friend, someone, somewhere, somehow knows where the—your Magi chalice plate is actually located. It is near to a place called, Saqqara, that's the step pyramids not too far away, the owner says he would sell it to me for LE 1500—but, to me only.

That's about one hundred and fifty pounds sterling, Mr Hastings. The owner says there is great responsibility for the custodian of this article of faith and if the museum wants to take custody of the chalice, then he would be happy to part with it."

Kemp dropped his head in disappointment, the look on his face said it all. He knew that the Egyptian high commission kept strict controls of their archaeological history and getting an uncontrolled piece or artefact through customs and out of the country would be near damn impossible.

"Don't worry, Kemp, I will purchase it, and then present it to your Order as a gift. How does that sound? Now if you have the LE 1500 leave it with me, and I will ensure that you receive your new acquisition, and the documents to clear customs."

Hastings smiled a very broad smile, exposing his very white set of gnashers, and quizzed the Professor further.

Although he trusted him completely, he did not trust any outsiders, nor could he understand how such a strange an important artefact can be so readily available and located so quickly.

He surmised it was a case of just 'who you know' as opposed to what you think you know, and agreed to the transaction. Just then Kemp's mobile also flashed up, the word DARLENE indicated an incoming call. He clicked the green button and listened. "'Kemp, can you hear me? Bloody, phones; bloody Egyptians! Anyway, I am on my way, will be with you shortly. And tell me, why does every damn taxi driver toot their bloody horns every five seconds at me? Even the ones going the wrong way, morons that they are. I will see you in about fifteen minutes, unless I get taxi-jacked."

Kemp closed the phone and watched the great Professor Mohammed Elfecky at work. The Professor was running his fingers across every inch of the granite coffin lid. Kemp giggled as he watched Mohammed jump inside and outside the new sarcophagus, then inspect the sides of the casing as one would if purchasing a new car. Hastings smiled again.

"Moh! That thing is a couple of thousand years old, that's a lot of miles on the proverbial time clock, it is bound to have a few scratches!'

Twenty-five minutes later and Darlene arrived at the museum and introduced herself to Professor Elfecky. Hastings appeared to be excited again. He felt somehow responsible for Darlene's strange affliction and was never more than happy than when she was close by. Let alone being her chaperone in the land of sand and camel droppings, but not just on this trip, but in her life in general, but he was unsure exactly where their relationship was heading.

"What a nice looking woman," remarked Elfecky, who winked and made off into one of his many cupboards, searching for another book or artefact.

Kemp gave Darlene a huge smile. "Darlene, Mohammed has located the chalice for me, how efficient is that?"

She turned to the statue of Seth and smiled. "That's good news," she replied, then shook her head and wandered off out in the hallways casually making her way upstairs toward the gold jewellery and the gallery rooms.

"Take your time my dear, there is much to see, I will stay open just for you!" shouted Mohammed, closing the closet door.

"Hey you, slow down—you have two wives already; three would just put you in a sarcophagus like the rest of your friends."

There was another moment of humour and the two concluded their business and finished their drinks in a hail of laughter and jovial amusement. They were each remarking on one of their previous escapades together.

An adventure and an encounter being one that almost had them both incarcerated for being too drunk to walk home and had somehow tried bribing the duty police officer to drive them both to the museum. In their drunken state they both fell asleep in the temporary tomb exhibit of Seti the III and were nearly entombed as the exhibit was being prepared for transit.

The Silent Apostle II

Hastings endured another cup of Nile residue and paid the good Professor for his assistance in acquiring the 'magi chalice' and made out a receipt—in the name of the museum—then handed over the agreed LE 1500.

"Deal done, my friend," exclaimed Mohammed, who placed the money in the Museum's safe.

Chapter Six
The Assignation of Worlds

Twenty-five minutes earlier and three hundred shops later, Darlene had arrived at Tahrir square and then walked through the upper galleries of the Cairo museum. It was quieter than quiet and the warm air wafted through the many sarcophagi and caught her olfactory senses unaware, causing her to take many deep breaths, almost becoming light headed at one point.

"Wow, the jasmine is very strong, and the vanilla very sweet," she muttered, as she entered the papyri room and walked on through the alley and in to the gold room, stopping momentarily to view the row of sarcophagi that stretched the length the chamber.

Darlene, took quite a bit of time and quizzed the many marble or granite tombs' inscriptions; the ancient coffins standing in their capacity as testament to the ancient trade of masons and stone workers, let alone undertakers and the embalmers, each having left their many marks as specialist tradesmen, in the art of death.

They were the elite, those who applied their secret skills toward death and its very complicated Egyptian ritual subject matter. There was a sudden clatter that resonated through the museum. She flinched and jumped as the heavy wooden shutters downstairs were closed and echoed a series of clunks across the open void spaces of the chamber. Each security shutter was being closed by the night wardens.

It was the heavy clunking of the matt shuttering surfaces coming together that had startled her momentarily. Hastings, meanwhile, was beginning to make his way up the heavy marbled stairway and was en route to take another look at the mask of the greatest golden face in human history: the great young boy King, Tutankhamen, and to take an opportunity to talk and walk with his assistant.

The boy King waited patiently in his glass case and still maintained his superiority and status of his Kingship, even in death after almost four thousand years in the waiting, as the face that was never to be forgotten. But at this special moment in time, he waited for the arrival of Kemp Hastings to gaze upon his golden shroud.

There was another series of 'clunks' then the vocal mumblings of the duty guards echoed across the museum as they set the heavy steel locks into place, and confirmed with the words 'maya, maya'.

Darlene stopped and thought for a moment, acknowledging that there was no imminent hurry, there were no races within these walls, there were no time scales to be adhered to, and she observed that neither of the four men appeared to be over eager to complete the task in any record timescale.

Darlene had halted her walk about on the second level and was busy staring into the face of an ancient 'el Greco' Grecian mummy, whose beautiful face had been painstakingly hand painted onto the flat surface of the mummified bandages.

It was an attempt to show the unsuspecting modern world of the future, what the interred lady actually looked like, and could be a true resemblance. Darlene thought about the painstaking detail in order to preserve the image of life in death.

She stared for quite some time as she quizzed the eyes of the adjacent mummy; something about the face was intriguing, and comforting, although she knew they lived four thousand years apart. The interred mummified lady had good strong features, clean fresh eyes, a strong jawline, an unblemished skin tone and very fine red hair, but Darlene could not quite place the face she was staring at.

She recognised it, but suddenly struggled to place exactly where she had seen the woman before, especially in her capacity as a historical studies scholar, and she remained cognisant and understanding—knowing full well that this mummy was perhaps well over three thousand years old.

Another loud 'clunk' rang throughout the halls of the museum as the lower shutters of the remaining windows were fully locked and in place. Professor Mohammed Elfecky had cleared his desk and was busy signing off the staff rota sheet for the weekend—having made his investigation of the new acquisition.

It was going to be another record attendance this weekend as the museum had recently procured these new artefacts from lower Saqqara and two new mummies for public display. The management team were expecting a VIP visit from the good Doctor Hawas himself and the team were very excited.

Darlene, meanwhile, moved to the next display case and ran her fingers slowly across the front panel of the glass case. The cabinet sat adjacent to the case that contained the painted faced mummy which contained the remains of what was thought to be another Greek Queen, and, paused for reflection thinking as to what her own appearance would look like if portrayed in this manner.

She pondered on what would her image look like if she were to be embalmed or had been subjected to cryogenic storage in death, and how modern technology would preserve her body and more importantly her stunning looks. It was then that her fertile mind started to wander off again and run amok into the world of embalming. The room temperature had suddenly changed from being moderately warm to actually getting very warm, just as Darlene slipped into a trance and experienced a 'dream from hell'.

It was several minutes later when Hastings found Darlene standing in the upright position and she was still gripping both sides of the crystal glass case, holding herself in place. She appeared to be clearly frozen or traumatised and was still staring directly into the 'el Greco' inhabited display case.

Hastings gingerly touched her shoulder; she was absolutely rigid solid to the touch. He flinched, and momentarily pulled his hand back. It was as if her muscles had gone into some sort of acute spasm. He then stepped to one side of the glass case and observed Darlene's face from an opposing angle. He flinched again and felt very uneasy as he stared directly into her beautiful green eyes—they were fully dilated and very dull. He then reached out again and touched her hand, her skin was pallid.

If Kemp was to place a bet, he would say that Darlene was in a state of shock and that her body fluid had stopped circulating, but was somehow still stabilised. Reaching up, he placed his hand over her forehead and flinched as the motionless fingers were as cold and as solid as her torso was.

"Oh shit, shit, shit and shit!" he exclaimed, whilst rapidly making his way across to the central main balcony, immediately above the regal entrance of the museum, and shouted over the top of the marble post at the top of his voice in order to grab Dr Elfecky's attention.

Mohammed had instantly appeared from his office and was staring up at Hastings from the centre point on the ground floor, almost standing in the middle of the great circular motif that dominated the lower rotunda granite flooring, where the concentric balcony reached around and towered well above him in mirrored image above.

"What is it Meester Hastings?" he shouted, whilst simultaneously grabbing and placing his black rimmed glasses back on the bridge of his nose. He recalled how Kemp had christened the heavy rimmed optics earlier in the year as 'NHS' glasses.

He had almost forgotten how Hastings had commented on the thickness of the lenses so long ago, which somehow for Mohammed made him feel more like a British academic as opposed to an Egyptian one. But he revelled in the 'learned' change of his appearance, and how he was being perceived by others as an eminent boffin.

"One moment please, Mister Kemp, I am just adjusting my 'bottle bottoms'. I cannot see without them you know," he said, and continued to stare up at the balcony.

Kemp responded in an even louder voice. "Hurry, please, get up here, jaaldi jaaldi (hurry) it is Darlene she is, well she is . . . I do not bloody know, something very strange—just get up here!"

A few moments later the very tired and panting Doctor Elfecky found an almost distressed Kemp Hastings staring at the motionless, upright body of Dr Darlene Gammay from very close quarters.

"Well, what do think of this, situation?" asked Kemp, wiping his chin, which had somehow become splattered in tiny droplets of saliva. Mohammed took some time to look Darlene over then shook his head. Kemp gave him a very odd gaze as if he suspected something was not quite right with the Professor, his mannerisms had seemed to have changed. Hastings dismissed this is a thing of the moment—given the nature of their encounter.

"Well, Mister Kemp, I am absolutely buggered if I could explain her current mental condition, but her physical condition, well it appears to me as if she is in a stasis or a limbo condition." The Doctor took a deliberate pause then delivered his thoughts as an academic. "Kemp, she appears to be comatosed or in a very deep sleep."

Hastings drew his left hand threw his hair and grimaced. "I can see that, but how the hell on God's earth did she become to get in such a state. Have you been spraying some sort of sleep drug or pesticide in here, she could be suffering from some sort allergic reaction?"

Elfecky suddenly turned left and took flight, disappearing into one of the adjacent chambers and began scanning the many papyri documents that were encased in the ancient documents section of the room. Each dossier had been placed in order of date and precedence, some of which were segmented into categories, of ritual and afterlife, and just one of the 130,000 articles that the museum boasted.

The huge library of papyri had been chronologically placed in sequence and readily identified, according to the many dynasties in succession, and of which was easy for anyone wishing to find a particular language or script in time to locate and view.

Kemp could actually do nothing at all, but decided to just stand and stare at Darlene from his standpoint, whilst simultaneously watching Professor Elfecky who was now very cautiously walking between the many display cases whilst running his fingers and his mature well-seasoned analytical eyes over the many scripts.

After about three minutes he stopped, then extracted a set of old, brown, rusty, tarnished keys from his pocket, then began shuffling a single key in the lock to the cabinet. Kemp meanwhile, smirked, almost smiling as he observed the Mickey Mouse key fob dangling downwards from the small chain, just as the cabinet sprung open.

It was then that the Doctor turned and faced Hastings his eyes were almost dilated to full glare and he appeared to be very excited. "'I have it, I have found it, I knew it was here, look, look come see," he exclaimed, holding the parchment high up in the air.

"Have what? You mad, deranged, Egyptian scientist," responded Kemp, almost sprinting forwards to grab the papyrus and absorb the secret information. Of course, knowing full well it would be absolutely futile as his knowledge of Arabic was somewhat basic, and he would simply be lost amongst its text.

He often had to rely on his peers such as Mohammed to explain what was written upon ancient documents, and now this old parchment, of which he was desperate to understand and assist Darlene in her moment of need, and presently could do absolutely nothing to help her.

"This, my friend, is the secret Gnostics Mystical ritual of 'live' embalming,' responded the Doctor.

"What?" exclaimed Kemp, almost shuddering in disbelief on hearing Elfecky's comments.

"Live embalming!" he exclaimed again.

"Are you off your archaeological rocking trolley Mohammed? How in God's name could you have come to make such an arsehole assumption as that?" quizzed Kemp, who was almost clenching his fists in total anger and frustration as he reached out to grab the manuscript.

"Oh, that's quite simple, Mr Hastings, we have it documented in the Mystical Circle's paperwork," answered the good the Doctor as he clasped the septum of his nose, then pointed to several incision marks that had appeared on Darlene's pale skin. Each mark appearing as a single red scar at her neckline and ear lines.

These incision marks were indicators that were very evident on Darlene's motionless upper torso, as she remained standing in the upright position whilst traversing the lands of limbo in her mind, and yet she was still grasping the side panels of the glass cabinet, albeit frozen in the moment of time.

Doctor Elfecky pulled out his pencil and pointed to specific areas of the body whilst explaining that if these areas on the body were cut with surgical precision, then they could stimulate the human brain responses, and in essence telling the brain to shut down into a state of limbo. A physical process, when executed correctly, would increase the levels of melatonin in the body having induced the body's natural defence mechanism to function, therefore, actually tricking the unsuspecting brain to close down and go to sleep.

Professor Elfecky went on to explain similar actions that were common place actions today in some surgical techniques. "As one does when twisting a horse's nose or rubbing and caressing the underside of a salmon—a process used in order to momentarily make beasties vulnerable," explained the Doctor in greater detail, whilst still pointing out the incision marks on Darlene's skin. Hastings was flummoxed, astounded even, as he glanced at the parchment and then back at Darlene.

Dr Elfecky began explaining the ritualistic mechanics of the embalming procedure. "'In essence, Kemp, to preserve a body in preparation for the afterlife which can be a long and arduous process for the embalmers—normally a group of skilled tradesmen will take forty days and nights to prepare a single corpse for ascending into the heavens.

It was in the latter period of ancient times that we, as a nation, had started to inter our dead in coffins, as it was soon discovered during sand burials that the remains were often dug up and eaten by the animals of the desert.

But as time progressed the many coffins became more and more complicated depending on the wealth that a family was prepared to spend on the remembrance process. Even then, the many bodies which had been placed in coffins also decayed, that was even if they were not exposed to the hot, dry arid sands of our deserts.

It took several centuries before nomads who hailed from the village of Mumy had found and practised the art of preservation, where the dead remained almost life like even after some time in death. The process was almost described as pickling a corpse, but using special oil recipes and linen strips thinly applied to build up a layer after layer of protection, as opposed to just applying vinegar. But where many layers were cut thin enough to keep the features of the face clear and intact, as you know this is what we deem mummification or embalming."

Hastings interjected. "Yes, but Moh, you said 'live' embalming—surely that sounds like more of a macabre type of ancient torture rather than a process of preservation?"

The Doctor smiled. "Indeed, Kemp, but that only depends on how you view your particular religion. Surely don't you think that receiving the wounds of Christ is equally as disturbing as being embalmed, alive or otherwise, as no-one is quite sure of the outcome, often as not . . . in other rituals, the recipient eventually dies."

Kemp took an over dramatised deep breath whilst running both hands through his hair again. "Okay? Then what does that parchment say about our current state of affairs concerning Darlene. Does it explain how to bring her out of this state of mind or what?" he said, pointing directly at the manuscript and wiggling his finger.

The Professor scrunched up his face and huffed a little, he was contemplating what to do next, and clearly caught up in either the confusion of the moment, or he had a plan of action. Hastings convinced himself not to hold his breath for any decisive actions, as this was after all Egypt.

"Well, if my assertions and understanding are correct, Darlene has been chosen, or singled out to either receive a 'calling' which can be indicated by receiving 'non-incorruptibility' or corruptibility status. Basically meaning that when she dies she will either be preserved or she will not, but only when she is in her deathly state. Or conversely, which is more my train of thought is that she is actually handing something back to its original owner."

Kemp was instantly thinking that Darlene's tattoo was the obvious choice. Kemp nodded in agreement and started to explain how Darlene had received her biblical tattoo 13 days ago and that a strange series of events had ensued since that day. He explained the advent of the 'Sanctos Epistula' or holy parchment again, that was rumoured to have been written and illuminated by Mary Magdalene herself, and the incredible journey the manuscript had endured up through the ages into modern times, and had indeed survived the great fire of London in 1666.

Where the world around it's colourful page had been simply incinerated. Hastings also explained the series of inexplicable events regarding the Hell Fire Sword itself, and the theft of Dante's painting of the Sank Real, and not forgetting that the Pope himself had endured the visions and visitations that Darlene had received prior to him having suffered a fatal heart attack in vault 33 of the Vatican's secret museum.

Elfecky was mesmerised, even he thought that this event was somewhat unbelievable but had heard of similar accounts elsewhere and commented earlier during their discussion, a revisit of the same event, and yet only having occurred as recently as the 19th century in France, Ethiopia and India.

The Professor sneezed, three distinct sneezes and wiped his face then started to explain how the process of the afterlife was conducted. "Alright, Kemp, let me

The Silent Apostle II

explain the open ritual of mummification in quick mode. The corpse is re-located to a subterranean chamber under what we will call a pyramid. Prior to this, the body is laid out in state in a simple tent called an 'IBU' this is basically a cleaning and purification station, where oils and palm wines are used to smooth the body and keep it smelling nice, having been rinsed with the waters of the Nile.

Remember earlier we talked about cuts and precise incisions, well this is when the embalmers will cut down the left side of the corpse and remove the internal organs. But this is where Darlene's condition differs. Come look here," he said, pointing to the detail on the papyrus. "According to this GMSC inscription, or what I can see, is a direct reference to the book of the Dead. Darlene is in an actual condition or 'dream state'. She is enduring non-physical or hypothetical surgery."

Kemp raised his hands in total disbelief. "Stop, stop, stop, you are rambling, Moh!" he exclaimed again. "Are you saying Darlene is enduring surgery in some sort of magic happy 'hippy' trip in this ethereal plane, place?"

Mohammed turned the papyrus over and pointed to a few sketches which displayed a small hieroglyph that depicted the process being conducted by several heavily gold clad ornate priests and priestesses. It was clear that no physical metal tools or surgical instruments were being used, but clearly a range of smaller flowers, lotus leaves and various other foliage and fruits had being substituted for things like surgical scalpels, PM 4O precision cutting tools, knives and needles, normally used in the modern day by specialist morticians as post mortem technical instruments.

Elfecky continued with his explanation and passed the parchment to Hastings for further scrutiny. "The organs decay first, so quite naturally they are first to be removed. But did you know, Meester Hastings, that each organ has a custodian in the afterlife?

A deity or notional person who is accountable for the lungs, liver, guts, and even the small and large intestines are washed then repacked in a mixture of natron and oils—this stage of embalming will dry the organs out thoroughly. However, at this stage our physical heart remains in situ to the very end of the process as it is deemed our 'centre of intelligence'."

Just then, Kemp started thwarting a couple of flies that were intent on making his life a living beastie hell, and just would not give up on their unrelenting attacking efforts to give him a bite or three. It was a situation of Egyptian life where he had no choice but to endure the beasts and keep swiping the little blighters away, and had continued to swipe them since his arrival in the land of the Pharaohs; the land where flies are Kings and ever present.

Mohammed waited patiently until he had settled down—having mortally wounded a single fly in his swatting efforts. Then the Professor continued in his lesson. "Of course we as a living entity require our hearts in the afterlife and that's why this special organ is the last one to be disturbed, because, during the ritual of afterlife preparation we must keep the two close together as long a practically possible."

Kemp was wholly amused and could not stop glancing back and forth at Darlene, wondering what she was actually witnessing or feeling in the rather bizarre and complicated unseen process she was captured within.

Clasping his hands and momentarily pursing his lips Mohammed took a few seconds and quizzed the frozen

Doctor again. "She will not feel discomfort or any pain, just as the ritual text here explains, but, then again, I am only reading this straight extract from the document itself. It appears that from the perspective in the mind of the receiver, the complete process is over in a flash or moment in time."

Kemp began to squirm a little as Elfecky explained the use of the 'hooking' instrument that was used to 'mish-mash' the brain up into an intellectual mushy pulp. He absorbed in his mind's eye as the residue of off-white, milky warm cauliflower was splashing around deep up inside the cranial vaulted, bony cavity of his head. He shivered a little, as the Professor continued.

"Then, the pulpy CSF—cerebra spinal fluid—is mixed with what is left from the intellectual DNA—deoxyribonucleic acid, or thin blood—which is then forcefully extracted through the nostril cavities using a small set of ice-cream type scoops or spoons.

"Ouch!" exclaimed Kemp, almost falling over as he comprehended the actions of the skilled undertakers scooping the brains out of the head like smooth ice-cream from a solid tub.

"Steady, Kemp," retorted Mohammed, placing a hand on his shoulder—a quick catch in order to stabilise him from falling over. You think too deeply my friend, don't let your emotions get the better of you. Darlene is not feeling any pain or discomfort, to her it will be as if she can see everything but not feel the pains of the incisions or any organ removal.

You can think of it as that she has been given a one hundred percent huge epidural to stem any feeling, a type of astral anaesthetic injection for the brain, but her visions will be clear as day."

Kemp raised his hands again and spluttered out a few words. "How can you be so calm when you know that she is going through such hell and all this in her head Mohammed? Even in her mind's eye she will be traumatised."

The Doctor responded. "Yes, she will, but only for a glimpse into the afterlife, but she will also have been blessed with the gift of foresight as a result of this amazing process. I think what we are actually witnessing here is the complex process of an actual ancient and esoterical 'Assignation'.

Kemp, this is what the Apocrypha is all about; these are things you don't read about in the Bible or on any religious documentation. A process and passing over of a very mysterious transitional custody process of something that reaches well beyond your biblical proportions. Kemp, I really cannot answer any of your questions entirely one hundred per cent, because, this is only the second time this phenomenon has occurred. Well, that is according to this parchment, which incidentally dates well before the days of Christ and reaches back approximately 4,000 years, and I have no idea, of course, who wrote it.

But what I do know is that it is one hundred per cent authentic and most likely written by a High Priest under the watchful eye of the ancient Pharaoh at the time of the first Assignation. And, in case you are wondering, Mister Hastings, it's not entirely scripted in the Egyptian language either; there are odd symbols here and there, symbols that I am deciphering as either Aramaic or Hebrew."

The Professor responded whilst drawing his fingers over the rippled, tanned surface of the document again, "Then again it could be written ancient Assyrian or pseudo Babel as the two languages do look very familiar."

The Silent Apostle II

The Doctor paused and took time to view the document again then continued his lesson in embalming. "So, Kemp, let us continue with our whistle-stop overview and tour of embalming. Once the body is completely dried out, it is then washed again, and bathed in more oils. But this time the oily coating physically lubricates the skin which then remains like an elastic membrane.

Now, before you say it, and this is the important bit, if this process was executed in middle of Europe, the body would be immortalised or have been made almost incorruptible, but without the art of the embalmer it is almost inconceivable, and that is the real quandary that your church faith leaders must consider very carefully before announcing that the human remains of a deeply religious person is canonised or beatified in death.

Unless the bodies of the deceased are physically embalmed in Egypt then moved to a cooler climate then that transition could enhance the anointed properties. If it is a colder climate where the remains would be interred, then it stands to reason the process could be sustained indefinitely, but you know as well as I do, it is only the last couple of hundred years that this anomaly has come to light in Europe.

Anyway, once all the organs are removed they are then wrapped in a soft linen ball and normally placed back into the body, which by this stage had also been stuffed with leaves or sawdust and long soft linen pads, which were then coated with more sweet smelling oil or 'the oils of death'. Then finally wrapped completely with an outer shroud of linen.

If you take time to review the complete process, Mr Hastings, you will find that over the many years our embedded Egyptian religious beliefs have changed toward the afterlife and the understanding of heavenly travel.

Our ideals and thinking towards death has evolved—and now, we find that the organs are placed in canopic jars once removed from their host. These jars or cups were normally made of wood, but more commonly we see alabaster or thin clay jugs are used—it is all dependent on how rich your family actually were.

But, we do find, in some cases, that the organs have been placed back into the body and the canopic jars remained in the shrine as a symbolic container for viscera, these are containers for afterlife protection. And finally, Mr Kemp, our organs: the liver, heart lungs, etc., all important elements for existence in the after world, must be kept together.

Take the liver as an example, an important organ for the afterlife the designated god 'Imsety', or the human headed god, is the liver's custodian, and we also have 'Hapy', the baboon headed god, and of which the air that we breathe belongs to him and, so do our lungs. Whilst last, but not least, Qebehsenuef or the falcon headed god, has custody of our intestines.

And that, Mr Kemp, is in reality the physical side to the very complicated art of embalming. How do you feel now? You do not look well at all," asked Elfecky, removing his glasses and giving them a wipe with his well-used handkerchief.

Kemp was nodding nonchalantly and would be the first to have said: 'I am fine, I can deal with trauma, blood, shit, feathers and gore.' But Hastings knew his olfactory senses were telling him otherwise; he was overcome by the sweet smell of almonds and warm blood. He looked up, just as his head started swirling inside, he was consciously nauseous and dizzy, and he could feel himself losing the sensation in his legs and he started swaying again.

Mohammed, meanwhile, had caught the attention of one of the guards and was shouting. "Maya, maya—barraka, maya minfadluk!"

One of the guards ran off into an anti-chamber in an effort to get some water A few moments later and Ashraf, the door guard, had brought back a bottle of sparkling water which Kemp suddenly grabbed out of his hands and consumed in three straight gulps, then apologised for his hasty and unprecedented actions. "Shukran, shukran, thank you," he repeated.

Mohammed, in the meantime, had been simultaneously aware that Doctor Darlene had twitched a couple of times in response to something or other in her Assignation journey to and from the netherworld. This was combined with the fact that a few tears had formed at the corner of her eyes and were slowly running down her pale white cheeks. It was clear to the Professor that she was emerging from her psychological unearthly trip.

Doctor Elfecky continued to observe her condition and had correctly anticipated Darlene falling backwards on to the cold stone floor as she returned to what may have seemed normality from her induced sleepy state.

Mohammed had been quick to respond and did indeed judge his timing precisely as he caught the Doctor as she toppled backwards still in the upright posture as her body failed to defy gravity and was pulled to the floor.

Her internal organs had started to vibrate and come back to normal working condition and were responding to the blood flow as it started to course and pulse back through her heart and into her veins and around the remainder of her body. Her circulatory system was in overdrive. A single squeal and she had begun writhing around on the floor like someone having an acute fit and a few jerks of her legs then she appeared to shake and shiver with cold.

Kemp was motionless. He knew how to deal with diabetics in the straight who were craving insulin or their chocolate craving, but he had no idea how to react as Darlene twitched and jerked in a very sporadic, un-uniformed manner.

A full minute of hysteria and things had suddenly settled. Darlene had stopped shaking, then out of the blue she shot bolt upright, still in the sitting position and started ripping at her shirt, screaming that her back and shoulders were burning or were on fire. Kemp placed both hands on her shoulders and started to massage her neckline. In response, the Doctor ripped half of her blouse clean off, leaving the remnants of cloth to cover up her right breast and what was left of her bra strap as she continued to struggle with her clothing.

Doctor Elfecky had momentarily turned up again. Kemp had not noticed he had disappeared during the bout of confusion, but had brought back some water and his little black bag of tricks. His bag contained quite a myriad of pots and a range of coloured bottles and little jars that contained just what the Doctor had not ordered: a fine opium extract.

A quick injection and Darlene had been subdued to a manageable state. Kemp continued to keep Darlene warm and comfortable and had noticed that her tattoo had in fact completely disappeared and that the majority of her back was inflamed with acute red or inflamed bruising but he remained mindful that Darlene had not been physically harmed. He certainly could not apply the same diagnosis to her psychological state of mind.

Within an hour or so, the three were sitting in Doctor Elfecky's home discussing the day's very odd events. Darlene was now fully bright as a button and back to her normal active, humorous state as if nothing had happened and was engaged in healthy conversation. Kemp and Mohammed remained very sceptical but remained interested and monitored her condition should she suffer a relapse.

Kemp placed a warm cup of caramel and chocolate coffee in front of her, then asked her about her time in the museum. "So, Darlene, this is going to sound a bit odd, but we thought you had died there and then in the upright position. If it was not for Dr Elfecky's quick witted thinking I would have had you in an ambulance and away to Cairo Central Hospital for treatment in a jiffy."

Darlene placed both hands on her cup and gingerly sipped her drink. "Kemp," she said, softly. "I had the weirdest dream of unworldly sensations. It was just after I thought I had bumped my head against the glass panel of the display case but, huh, that was just the beginning. From what I could gather, I was actually physically frozen as I watched the 'Anubis' the Egyptian god of embalming, who had begun making some sort of ceremonial preparations. After a few minutes, I was trapped somehow immobilised. Then I could feel my body slowly tighten up all over.

My mouth was suddenly very dry, I had shootings pains starting to run up through my back and my head, I could feel the pressure begin to build up behind my eyes, oh, it was horrible, and for one moment I thought I had lost control of my normal human bodily functions, it was really scarey.

Then I started to struggle and pant for breath and I mean really struggle for breath, I was literally choking. My mouth felt as though it was being prised open against my will, and my lungs felt as though they were being ripped out. Then I took another single, very deep, and I mean deep breath, when I suddenly found myself lying on my back facing upwards.

I was laid out flat on a cold, solid bed. I could feel a raffia work frame work of matting with a single ridge that ran the length of my spine digging into my back, and it seemed to arch upwards near to the nape of my neck, then two pads were placed under my buttocks and it was bloody uncomfortable, not painful, just a discomfort.

I could actually see many people walking around me, lots of individuals moving in and around my body carrying jars and bottles and funny instruments, they were Egyptians I think, they dressed like Egyptians but I could not be quite sure, and there were also a few older men amongst them, I have no doubt about that, as they all had donned blue and gold ceremonial headgear and possessed very wrinkly faces. Several of them were walking around the room singing and chanting whilst casting some sort of white powder all over my body.

I definitely felt six warm patches at my ear line and my neckline, and I felt as though my ankles and wrists had been, well, what I can only describe as being cut or slashed. But no pain was evident, just a warmth as I slipped from consciousness into a mellow chilled kind of lazy state, but I remember thinking that I was being drained of blood. I know this all sounds bizarre but to me it really happened. I then noticed directly above me was a single woman, she was leaning over me and smiling, a very beautiful women with red hair, and, oh, Kemp, not too unlike the face on my tattoo. That much I do remember in fact almost the same facial structure.

But her hair was more cropped, and her eyes were more piercing, what I do recall was that above her head, painted on the vaulted roof, was a line of fishes, like the ones you find in reference to your Fisher Kings—you know, the one before religion actually took its iron fist grip, the fish and the letters 'IR' next to it, that 'Jesus' Rex' inscription, just sort of running in a freeze around the room. God that was weird."

Darlene stopped talking and paused for a moment, then crunched up part of her blouse and showed Kemp the top muscle of her left shoulder. "Is it still there?" she asked, expectant of an answer that would ease her many fears. Her worst thoughts being that perhaps she had accumulated yet another unwanted holy gift from the Lord above.

Kemp pulled the desk lamp nearer to the seat and started nodding. "Oh, Darlene, it looks as if it has gone, thank God," he exclaimed. "Looks like it's only very slight bruising now, but there is no huge tattoo. It's definitely gone, Darlene, but there is a small black cartouche at the nape of your neck."

Darlene took a very big deep breath and let out a sigh of relief. Kemp, meanwhile, had grabbed his Blackberry and took a quick snapshot, and then showed the digital image to her. She gazed at it then closed her eyes again.

Doctor Elfecky, on the other hand, was sitting across the room watching the couple with the keenest of interest, quietly absorbing the strange circumstances he had found himself inextricably linked within. Then he spoke out,

"You two would make quite a perfect item. Although I know that you are not together biblically—you know what I mean? Yet you both seem to trust each other implicitly, and that's very nice to see." He stood up and opened up the little, octagonal cupboard in the corner. "Brandy anyone?" He then smiled a huge Egyptian smile.

Hastings smirked. "You bet, yer big, bulbous, Egyptian arse Mohammed—brandy is always good."

Darlene almost started to cry and Kemp struggled to fight back his relief that the Doctor had not been struck down dead by some mishap or some strange ungodly act—let alone from a strange God. Darlene momentarily opened her eyes and continued to recite her experience in a mix of emotional burble and whimper.

Kemp leaned over and handed her his handkerchief, then she continued in her explanation of her experience. "After the woman appeared, it was then that something I observed really frightened the crap out of me, and I felt myself being both nauseous but not to the point of vomiting.

The instrument that was raised at my eye line was a long silver blade, it looked clean almost hygienic. But when my eyes fully focussed, I could see that she had held up a large, long knife with a pin point hook at one end. It was sort of like an Ankh shape but a lot more open at the hook end, between a shepherd's hook and a long Ankh.

It was then that I could feel my nose streaming fluid and my ears had gone numb with what felt like pins being slowly pushed in to my inner ear, and my eyes were watering, and I mean watery, but there was no sense of acute discomfort or pain, more like having your body numbed and being moved around like a dead pig. It was then that I was aware that my hands were being tied, clasped together and linen strips wrapped around the wrists very tightly.

Then followed by each finger being pulled and fully extended with linen finger wraps placed on each digit and my toes. I had begun to panic as it suddenly struck me that I was being embalmed and there was nothing I could do, and clearly in mind I was still alive. I could hear my heart beat louder and louder almost drum like and, then it suddenly fell silent.

Then I saw my lungs, my liver and what I thought were my intestines being removed, each organ held up in front of my eyes to bear witness to—it was horrible. My arms and legs by this time had been wrapped separately and I could see trinkets being placed across my face, my stomach and my naval, I clearly heard the words: "The Isis knot" being spoken, as the woman conducting the ceremony seemed to chastise someone for not having it ready.

The Isis knot being a protective amulet, and the plummet amulet being the piece that keeps the balance of life and death in the afterlife. It was at this point I swore my eyes and ears seeped blood and my hair appeared to grow in mass quantities. I could see it slowly growing over my face then it went totally dark. Then instantly bright again, as if the lights had just been switched back on.

The woman was joined by what I could only think was a High Priest. He carried a large Ankh and waived a blue, long tailed flail with all other bits and pieces of trinkets and amulets over my eye line, as if I was supposed to acknowledge what he was doing. He had red eyes and was bald with a single band of gold that ran around his head like a crown. He was murmuring incantations from the book of the dead and had done throughout the complete process as I could hear the dull tones of his voice in the background, but, then I could see his face.

The Priest had tucked a single papyrus scroll between my hands and I could feel each letter of the hieroglyphs as if they were being literally burnt into my back and shoulders. There was a moment where my back and shoulders felt as if they were literally on fire, and absolutely scalding hot and burning, as if the skin was being peeled back off the muscle and bone by a heat gun, not unlike peeling wallpaper from the walls of a house with a domestic blow torch. I could feel all the bandages really tighten up when they poured syrup or oil on to the linen strips."

Doctor Elfecky interjected. "It was resin and palm oil. The resin protects and bonds the linen together, whereas the palm oil keeps the smell of death and decay at bay."

Darlene cast Elfecky a snide and an unwelcome grimace. "Well, Mohammed, that may be so, but with the utmost of respect, you can stuff that straight up where the Heliopolis sun does not shine. I was being painted and trussed up like a chicken for Christmas dinner and I was totally aware of what was going on, and that I was not dead. Albeit I was somehow being mummified, and you can trust me, I am not going to be forgetting that too quickly, that much I can assure you of. It was bloody frightening.

That was of course up until the lady leaned over and kissed my lips, and that is not something I am accustomed to, and you can trust me on that, and then I drifted off into a deeper sleep," she said, then lowered her eyes away from Kemp in almost embarrassment who was still clasping her hand whilst listening intently to her story.

The Egyptian Doctor acted as if he had taken no offence at all. He then stood up and asked if he could translate the cartouche on Darlene's neck. Darlene agreed and pulled her long, red hair to one side. The Doctor took a couple of seconds then opened his hands in almost praise.

"Oh, in the name of Allah!" He was almost shouting out in shear excitement. "This is the cartouche of the Great God Isis and complimented with Osiris—this is not common as they are combined together, written as one entity."

Darlene flicked her hair back over her neck line and drunk more of the cold brandy. "Yum, anymore?" she asked. "So what does that mean? This cartouche that contains both names?"

Elfecky smiled then spoke. "Basically, Darlene, it indicates one partnership but, two gods."

As the trio conversed, Doctor Elfecky's email and phone had flashed and bleeped in unison. And after a quick review of the incoming mail he sat down with his laptop and showed the wide colourful screen to Doctor Gammay.

"Darlene, when you were in the museum you appeared to be somehow mentally removed from reality and attached to this one mummy. The one that sits adjacent to theGrecian Queen. But do you remember what the actual face looked like before you placed in this trance?"

Darlene answered almost spontaneously. "There was no image on that particular mummy. I remember saying to myself: 'How can you tell who is who under death's dark veil'." Darlene wiped her brow and leaned forward, then carried on in her explanation.

"But, the next cabinet down from that one, well, that mummy had a very distinctive face and was clearly painted in the same style as the El Greco one, and it was a female. It was painted in a sort of Pre-Raphaelite Romanesque style—you know Rossetti, Caravaggio or Preti, that kind of painting.

I think I mean an El Greco painted face, and the third cabinet down, that was certainly a man's face that much I am certainly sure of, and when I think about it more, it could have even been the face of that High Priest I saw. I cannot be a million per cent sure, but it was close. I know this sounds very bizarre but if you had been through what I have endured, bizarre is acceptable—trust me."

Doctor Elfecky was nodding in agreement as he quizzed Darlene's facial expressions, and was trying his hand at interpreting her body language and even applied a few odd suggestion techniques. He was unsettled in his mind as Darlene portrayed every idiosyncrasy as if she was telling the truth, and he would agree with any professional that Darlene Gammay firmly believed that she had lived through the embalming process.

"Well, Miss Gammay, I fear you may have been part of something that we thought was always an ancient spiritual gnostic myth of rumour, you see we, as Egyptians, feel that although we believe that we can ascend into the heavens and stars, we do not think that we could actually return back to earth, you know like a return ticket to meet the Gods, or indeed let alone, pass on one's earthly image.

Therefore, the actual ritual process of passing on one's earthly image from death to life is what we deem, or more over, what is only known by a select few members of a very esoteric and inner circle of informed scientists, this is called the process of '**Assignation**'.

This is a journey to and from the afterlife; which is indeed a serious conundrum for us to consider. And I can assure you, Doctor Gammay, that 'we' as a relics and religious study group have no real examples of what this process entails or what it is really all about—apart from a few snippets of information which appears to have been hastily written on a few loose pieces of papyri that basically dwells on the notion that the transition is somehow real.

Of course that is until now, and you are now something of an enigma, not only to me, but to the collective 'the GMSC' institution. Apart from your own recent experience to compare with, this crossing over of human identities or this ethereal relationship between two worlds, I mean, it's just like passing on physical DNA.

The difference being one person is post physical birth and the other in death. The mummy that you were face-to-face with in the museum, the one you were drawn to, we actually have very little detail or indeed know very little about her. But it was known to be just the body a woman, and speculation was that she was perhaps a lesser princess or a high priestess in her own right.

We cannot confirm nor corroborate any identity because she could be a princess, albeit she could also be a simple lay person, so without her worldy riches with her, we could not identify her. But, what we have is a mummy who appears to have had 'no name' or at least our records show that there was no name offered or given to this particular mummy when she was first discovered, and, was thus, simply recorded with the next sequential number on the inventory list, and she is now known as number '33'. However, just recently we think we have found a parchment that you may be referring to.

A parchment that gives an indication that the mummy was relocated from nearer middle Egypt, but what is really interesting, is that we think she may have been named Miriam, Migda or Magidal, or a combination of both, but clearly written in the simple an older Aramaic script.

Now, if you wish to speculate and apply any informed opinion, that particular translation could be translated loosely into the European language name for Mary, Marie, Magdalena or Mary Magdalene and of course you also mention the papyrus scroll that was wrapped up in your hypothetical embalming.

But, please remain mindful, many girls of the ancient world were named Miriam. Well, the upshot is that the illuminated manuscript that plays a crucial role in identifying who she is, which is at this very moment in time is being hastily translated, and this is why I am not confirming anything because I am waiting on an email from a close academic friend.

Because, the piece of papyrus that was held by your so-called non-faced mummy was available when she was discovered, we were sceptical of its authenticity. Although we had a single clue, but it was deemed out of place as it was a much older than normal papyrus pages and was subsequently removed. The papyrus, along with the amulet, was placed in one of her accompanying canopic jars, and yes, that is also not quite normal practice. So, we are treading carefully before we tell the international community who she really could be.

But firstly, let me explain this email, by looking at these digital photographs it seems this mummy has also taken on a brand new face! This is the same mummy

The Silent Apostle II

you were with up until two hours ago that had no face on her coffin effigy. What is more frightening is that she may have acquired her old face back, we are unsure, we just don't know! I mean how on God's earth would you explain that to society in the modern day?"

Darlene and Kemp stared at each other for a good few seconds as Mohammed explained the context of his electronic mail. Kemp explained what he thought he had just heard Mohammed say. "Mohammed, step back a phrase or three, will you. Are you actually saying to us that the face that now appears on the mummy in question, by whatever means you wish to class it as, or by any stretch of the imagination, 'unusual' as it is as somehow been re-instated or painted back on the mummy?

Placed there by some inexplicable, unnatural phenomenon or inexplicable process that could be deemed 'a miracle of science', and believe it or not, now also appears to be the very same face that was reflected by Darlene's tattoo?"

"Yes, Kemp, that is exactly what I am saying."

The Professor spun around on his chair with a huge smile on his educated face. Then spun the laptop around for Darlene and Kemp to view the new image on the screen. Displayed, in full colour glory, on the laptop's wide screen it was clear that the same mummy was still lying offset in her upright open sarcophagus, and still encased in her glass display cabinet, and had taken on the facial appearance of Darlene's tattoo—if not the actual tattoo it was a very distinct likeness. And it possessed a quality of skin tone that was extremely detailed. Darlene pursed her lips and coughed, then mentally acknowledged the bright red hair of the mummy, then started to cry.

Kemp meanwhile was thinking about the humidity levels within the glass case and the different temperature changes that could have possibly dried out the bandages and some sort of paint reaction had occurred and perhaps the face had been there all along, but had been distorted by light. Or conversely he was thinking camera tricks. Nevertheless, Darlene was unconvinced about any other theory apart from the fact that she had carried this image on her skin and had passed it on.

Mohammed interrupted their conversation and continued. "Here look, and if this is correct, then it basically means that you have been identified as a custodian or assignee. She, this princess, could also have pre-written this scripture in her own hand. But, this is of course is just speculation because the mummy was discovered and recovered in the lower border's region near to the Gaza strip, and may have even been transported there after the fall of Jacob's Ford by the old world Knights' Templar from Jordan. Probably in the era leading up into the 11th or 12th century.

This mummy was moved there deliberately, along with some of the other golden trinkets and regalia that we now house in our museum, and, she was moved there for safety reasons. Darlene, you also mentioned that your mouth was forced open, this is indeed a holy ritual and permits the deceased to consume food and water in the afterlife. There are also occasions when the eyes are removed or are fixed open so that the soul can negotiate its way within the darkened pyramid structure as it's ascends the great gateway to the heavens."

Mohammed became somewhat very passionate in his recital and recollection of the recent acquisition and seemed to ponder on certain aspects in their moments of clarity. Kemp again listened with great interest and Darlene was traversing the room but listening very intently, only stopping now and again only to view the Professor's copious amounts of artefacts and to sip her brandy.

She recalled thinking that the Professor's house was probably more of a museum than the actual museum was. His life revolved around Egyptian history and he had become known as the alternate historian, as he preserved the cultural history of ancient Egypt.

Mohammed stood up and shook the parchment in the air like a fly swatter, then spoke. "The scroll, however, is of particular interest to us, as it was not uncommon to bury or entomb the dead with their worldly belongings and the scroll in reality was their actual letter 'Will and Testament' and is often used to today to decide who owns what items—a bit like the Rosetta stone but in parchment form. So, after all that embalming and concerted effort, we find that the body is ready for its journey through death or in your case, Doctor Gammay, life.

But, I do really feel you have been blessed with something more than just a simple coloured tattoo or this new cartouche signature. You see, in our belief system this process would be known as the '**Assignation**', a mark of acceptance that would propel one into an almost sainthood category, and, which may still await you, who knows."

There was a very painful moment of incredible silence that resounded around the small living space. Then Kemp spoke out. "Well, Darlene, let's face it, you are now something of an enigma and that issue we should not hurry and tell the world about too quickly. Life is far too short to have this event told to the outside world, or they, 'the establishment', would have you hidden away in some nunnery.

Or a sanatorium or other such place where the hands and heads of some strange and very inquisitive biblical scientists will only want to take blood and samples of everything else from your hair to your urine, and that's not happening." Darlene and Mohammed were nodding in agreement at each other. Then the professor spoke out. "Oh, and by the way, Kemp, I forgot to mention your chalice will be delivered by a Mister Ahmed Mohammed, El Ahmed, he says sometime Wednesday, I shall buy the artefact as agreed."

Kemp had totally forgotten about the Chalice in his efforts towards these new revelations that would have implications for his relationship with Darlene; it seemed somehow so insignificant with current affairs and he thanked the professor for his assistance.

Doctor Gammay held her glass up and asked Mohammed to refill it, then she dropped another bombshell. "Well, what about the huge black and ginger cats then? There were literally thousands of them running about this hypothetical chamber and one cat even sat on my chest, and I would swear that it spoke to me."

Elfecky stood frozen in his tracks still holding the crystal brandy decanter that was now hovering in mid pour. "Cats, what sort of cats, Miss Gammay?" he asked, whilst tilting his head upwards.

"Cats. Bloody big ones, you know, Felis silvestris catus, moggey mau, mouse catchers, that sort of cat!" She almost spurted at the line of questioning. "I don't really know, Moh, black, tortoiseshell and ginger but very large and I mean extreme. And they were immaculate; each was well groomed, not them all, but specific ones and were very clean, larger than normal sized eyes though, and others appeared to be totally untamed . . . but the big ones, they appeared to have significant standing in this environment."

Elfecky responded with an odd expression as Darlene continued talking. "I do know that cats keep vermin down and keep harvests in good order, but I reckon a thousand cats ran through the chamber as I began to feel a cold wind run through my legs and arms, and that was when you seemed to have stuck something in me."

Kemp spoke out. "We used drugs, sorry, but we had to do something. It was a mild opium extract, Darlene. We used it to ease the pain and stabilise you when we thought you were suffering an epileptic fit or something."

Darlene started to disagree. "No way, Kemp, I was not having any kind of mental fit. I was day dreaming for two minutes maximum, no longer."

Hastings tapped his black jewelled Rado watch. "Darlene, it was easy a full thirty-five minutes when you stood opposite that glass case. I know cus I timed it. I remember distinctly looking at my watch; it was roughly sixteen forty-five when you went up stairs as I recall, cus I was watching yo . . ." he cut himself short, then spoke again.

"Anyway, I was just finishing my dialogue with Mohammed here, and by the time I had massaged your shoulders, I momentarily spied my watch face and it was just after the quarter past the hour when you started to return to our time, if that's the correct words to use."

Darlene smirked another 'very not interested' type of female smug grin. Then spoke. "Cobra snakes! The cats were carrying cobras in their mouths, every single cat had a snake in its mouth, just thousands of them, they were not graceful or easy going, as some of these cats were, these ones were just biting the heads off and playing with the writhing torsos."

Professor Mohammed Elfecky rubbed the side of his head and removed his NHS glasses. Then interjected in order to vent his thoughts. "Darlene, snakes as you are probably aware also play a significant role in our society and even today as you have already stated cats still keep the vermin levels down.

In Egyptian culture we have a goddess called Mafdet, she is the deification of justice and execution and symbolised as a lion-headed goddess. But she could be interpreted as to controlling these cats which in essence are or were controlling the serpents, or the loose interpretation as the Gods controlling the unruly people, by discipline.

Not just controlling them but simply killing them as well by biting their heads off. The bigger cats themselves, well, they are slightly different, the Cat Goddess 'Bast' or 'Bastet' was her original name, and of which, through time was eventually replaced by the name Mafdet and this is the name we know her by today. But, again, her image was softened over time and is now the deity for protection, fertility and motherhood."

Darlene smiled. "Shit, Mohammed, I could have told you that! But why has the bitch picked on me to leave her mark on society? Your 'Bastet', your bloody deity, she has singled me out to conduct her quick Assignation with, I must admit this shit has seriously been sending me to crazy land, and you can be rest assured, I will not be stepping another foot back in your museum ever again.

And if you really want to know something scary, and then listen to this, there are twenty three other mummies up there in your museum that are able to see through and beyond their bandages and their glass display cases, and I do not want to be introduced to them ever again."

Darlene stood up and stared directly at Mohammed Elfecky who had been stunned by her strange revelations, and was sitting back in his chair almost pinned by Doctor Gammay's direct approach and strong dialogue as she continued in her moment of anger.

"They can hear, see, smell and if you listen hard enough you will hear their violent screams—demanding silence, or you will shudder when you hear their relentless pleas to be returned back to the sands of their ancestors. Mohammed, even in death your Kings and Queens cannot sleep."

Doctor Elfecky was totally displaced, and found it very difficult to comprehend what Darlene was saying. His eyes kept widening and his mouth dropped as each new revelation was conveyed by Darlene to his unsuspecting ears.

"And if you listen, you will hear those cats calling in the dark recesses of your museum, and they are not quiet either, the eighty five thousand or so that were embalmed then dispatched into the afterlife along with their masters. Well, they squeal twice as loud as their masters do, and you can trust me when I say that they are twice as big as they are on earth.

These cats are almost the size of mountain lions, and the mummies, well, from what I have just seen they are twice their earthly size as well. And you have an example of a wooden sarcophagus up in that museum, the one that is massive, well, that's about the right size in height, but only on the other side of your gateway to the afterlife, and thank goodness it's only 'ethereal.'

So, professor, doctor, mister museum curator or whatever it is you are, I do seem to have also travelled to yet another place in your Pharaonic lands, this place was definitely, called 'Beni Hasan', and if I am not mistaken it was known by the Gods of the day as the Land of the Feline or Cat City? Of course, I am only recalling these sound bites or distant echoes from my mind, but am pretty sure Cat City is correct. Mind you, I was somehow tripping the light fantastic at the time, so, how do you explain that Mohammed?" she implied, with a degree of control, then began throwing her arms up in the air like a two year old child frustrated by some newfangled toy.

"From what I can recall, I saw many, many cats all lined up in neat little rows, each one sitting next to each other and waiting to be fed, as if they knew they were to be fed by the Lords of the afterlife as a matter of course. It was as if each little animal knew its role in the afterlife, expectant of being looked after. Does that make sense to you? Each cat just waited patiently, then once it was fed, was then consumed by the sands of the desert.

It may be that these cats do re-appear after forty days and nights or later as with whatever ritual, and again, I suppose just waiting to be fed. Sounds like a cat's life to me. But, what was really interesting is that they spoke to each other in multi-tongue, not meow type cat speak tongue as you and I know it, but more phonetically; this was very clearly a structured language and something very different."

Professor Elfecky stood with his mouth slightly open and was mesmerised as the overwhelming level detail of the experience flowed from Darlene's recollection, just as if she had rehearsed the whole thing as an actor would their lines. He was not only confused but was intrigued as his scholastic and historical knowledge was not only being challenged but also corroborated at the same time.

He poured himself another strong brandy and sat down on the leather seat again and gazed through Darlene and beyond into the expanse of downtown Cairo. Outside the hustle and bustle was kept at bay, the Doctor had ensured that his home was both secure and free from unwanted noise pollution and had fitted double glazing in his doors which had heavy rubber seals. He had also taken time to ensure that he had installed controlled lighting, which was both electronic and natural, and he had taken great pains to ensure his own papyri collection was not subjected to any unwanted pollutants.

Darlene recognised bits and pieces of Mohammed's collection—mainly small, alabaster statues and some of the highly elaborate, gold leafed jewelry. She knew his collection would amount to quite a substantial sum of money if they were placed on the open antiquities' market, but in his defense Mohammed chose to keep his country's artifacts and gems in their rightful place of origin.

After a brief stay in Cairo, Kemp and Darlene along with their new 'magi chalice' were en route to visit the Grand Masters' Lodgings administrator and the museum's curator to review early Templar records regarding the role of the Magi during the birth of Christ.

Chapter Seven
Malta

Kemp and Darlene stepped down from the airbus 320 aircraft and took a slow pace down the aluminum stairway. The sun was almost blinding and the heat was stifling. Kemp shielded his eyes from the rays as he stepped off the bottom step and grabbed Darlene's hand in order to stable her as she stepped from the last tread.

They both then made their way to the airport terminal and passed through passport control. Soon, thereafter, they were booked in their hotel and were making plans for the next three days of fact finding. Kemp had arranged to meet the curator of the Cathedral Museum at M'dina and Darlene had arranged to do some serious shopping.

Two o'clock in the afternoon next day came quickly and Hastings soon found himself standing outside the museum of the Grand Order of the Knights' Templar, M'dina, and was waiting on his contact who happened to be the island's representative for the Fisher Queens in the United Kingdom.

He instantly recognised his contact as the red Porsche Carrera parked up in the designated car park space. Hastings finished eating his chocolate éclair and placed the wrapper in his pocket, then made his way to meet Graham Pinto De Souza of the Royal Order.

"Hey, Graham, nice to see you again. Thanks for making time for me this afternoon—really appreciate it."

De Souza, as far as Hastings was concerned, was something of an enigma in his own right. He represented what Kemp would call the inner sanctum of the Order and yet he possessed the intellect of a mad scientist. His broad shoulders and stature resembled Kemp's own size, height and weight, yet his maturity and stature was clearly established on a well-heeled and groomed individual.

"So, you asked about paintings of Caravaggio that carried any intimation towards a chalice or holy cup. But let us be quite clear here, Kemp, not the Holy Grail, just tell me you are not on some wild goose chase to see if we have it wrapped up in swaddling in our museum archives somewhere?"

Hastings gave out an uncontrolled bout of laughter as De Souza swiped his all areas electronic security pass. "No, I have tried that line already, but do we?"

The electronic gate swung open and Hastings and De Souza passed through. Unknown to him, his life's social and commercial details were flashing up on some hi-tech security database some three thousand miles away, and quizzed by one of its highly trained and technical operators.

Hastings was alerted by another presence in the hallway as a security guard pinned an 'Electronic 'Tag on his jacket's lapel.

"Okay," remarked De Souza. "Level two, here we come. Tell me, how long do you have here in Malta? We must do lunch whilst you are on the island, there is a really good restaurant in front of St John's co—cathedral, they do a great pizza.' He then turned left into an alleyway and ascended the marble stairwell.

"I am not sure if we have what you are looking for, Mr Hastings, have you tried reviewing Dante's collection in London? Dante was much more attuned to the works of the older masters and their hidden symbols, cups, vessels and the like, probably more than most contemporary artists of his day, artists who basically just copied the given subject matter. But Preti on the other hand, he has indeed left his mark on the face of the Temple across the globe.

He was indeed a visionary and far excelled the expectations of our progenitors. But Caravaggio, well, I must fall prostrate at his feet and indulge myself in his greatness of his artistic talents. As for Caravaggio he was a troubled genius, if you judge him by his account on canvas of the beheading of John the Baptist, you get the feeling that he actually could have been there as a witness. The illicit, graphic detail sends chills up and down my spine every time I gaze upon it."

Kemp smirked and followed De Souza up the circular stairway, every now and again touching the highly cleaned and polished brass handrail for support.

"You know Caravaggio was obsessed with Saint John and his turbulent life; spent all his years in acute study of the man and Saint, and had become an eminent boffin by all accounts, and a talented paint artiste, as well as you know. The skull downstairs is painted or reflected in one of his many paintings as it does in several temple masterpieces. All you have to do, Mr Hastings, is decide who the skull belongs to." De Souza smiled and touched his nose.

Chapter Eight
A date with death

The driver of the oncoming car sat bolt upright. His gaze was wide eyed and wholly fixed and concentrated one hundred per cent on the red haired woman who had just emerged into the quiet lane, and was about to step onto the roadway. She had been busy purchasing some gold from 'The Crown' jeweler's shop.

The driver, meanwhile, had waited patiently and watched until she had come back into his line of sight, then slowly picked up the momentum of the vehicle intent on striking the lady. He steered the heavy Range Rover directly toward Darlene Gammay just as she had taken her first step onto the roadway and began accelerating.

The red haired woman was instantly alerted by the sudden moment of something nearby and was cognisant of the car's sudden revving high engine noise and rapid movement. She had momentarily frozen and had somehow decided to ignore the oncoming machine.

The driver glanced in his rear view mirror then gripped the steering wheel with all his strength as he applied the full weight of his right foot down on the accelerator. He spied his own reflection looking back at him, he looked ill, indeed he was sick, a concoction of alcohol and drugs fuelled his suicidal attack on the unsuspecting shopper. He gazed over his forehead and hairline and then stared into his deep inset eyes.

Both of his eyes were littered with oversized blood capillaries, they were almost fully blood shot, and he smirked spying the once striking blue colour that had all but disappeared, dissipated into a heady mix of tiredness drugs and illness and hatred for the follower of Christ. But this was of no concern for him now—he was too intent on ridding the world of one example of the walking dead, and his mission was now almost complete.

The driver's bony hands were gripping the leather wheel and were now a real time, white knuckle ride where the indents of his phalanges and damaged skin began ripping as he grew tense and very impatient. As he gripped the wheel tighter, the ripped strips of skin on his hands became tarnished with copious speckles of blood droplets, each leaving long smears of red on the beige covering of the leather as he manipulated the wheel to straighten the car up for final impact.

His oily, rugged, tufty hair was ruffled and very unkempt. He knew he smelled bad and had not washed in a few days. But Ahmed Hasan Kabbal of the Grand Lodge of Cairo was not too concerned.

Darlene had spun towards her left side and caught sight of the oncoming driver and gave out a loud, high pitched squeal of surprise, spying the car coming toward her, dropping her pink hand bag in the process.

The driver had swerved again in order to strike the Doctor straight on, and, it was just then that a grey figure emerged from nowhere and grabbed Darlene Gammay's torso in a concentrated rugby dive sending them both hurling over the cobble stones and the cold slabbed walkway, in the process missing the steel bollard uprights by a mere few inches.

The Range Rover had simultaneously ripped through an adjacent steel bollard and veered off to the left hand side of the lane, and had started to descend the narrow stairway, smashing off the masonry and the many shop's front facades, sending fragments of chairs, plaster and glass flying into the air in the process.

The car had continued down over an intersecting street, luckily missing other traffic by inches and cascaded down over yet another set of stairs, then collided with a small curtain wall that gave way under the impact.

The last thing Darlene Gammay remembered was watching the number plate and the underside of the machine disappearing over the edge of the wall followed a loud clatter and a cloud of black smoke which bellowed up between the adjacent buildings.

Kemp brushed himself down then offered her a hand of help. "Really, can't leave you alone anywhere can I?" Came the welcome tones to Darlene's ears. Hastings had been her hero of the day, her man of the moment, her saviour. She was very confused and appeared to be very displaced by the event.

"I had just bought you this nice chain with a gold Maltese Cross on it as a present, when I . . ." she stopped. "Oh, my God, Kemp, that maniac just tried to kill me. Why would someone want to kill me?" she asked.

Having got to her feet they then followed the trail and destructive path of the Range Rover and soon found themselves descending to the narrow street below to view the carnage left behind by the mass of twisted metal.

Once they reached the flattened wreckage of the car, it was just as the flames had erupted into full glory as sparks and flame reached high into the sky and the aroma of petrol lingered heavily in the air which caught their olfactory senses. It was obvious that the car had flipped over and landed on its roof, then burst into flames.

He also noticed that the driver's seat was empty and stared around the immediate area for any signs of the previous occupant; no-one that remotely resembled anyone who could have been the driver was in the locality.

Everything in the open area was in normal order, apart from an old lady pointing her finger in the air and blurbing something about the darkened 'rains from heaven above' in half gargled Italian, and of course a one and half ton Range Rover sitting in a hail of fire and devastation in the middle of the small square.

"C'mon we need to get out of here and lie low for a little bit. How is your ankle, by the way?" asked Kemp, as Dr Gammay took a long deep breath.

"I will live, but I need new stockings."

They both smiled at each other and made their way back the hotel.

It was not long before there was a sudden knock on the apartment door which startled them both; it was a knock that was loud enough to wake the very dead.

Hastings instantly jumped up and peeped out of the 'spyhole' in the door whilst trying to remain calm. He was amazed to find standing at the other side was his long time Egyptian friend, Dr Mohammed Elfecky; he was standing and looking somewhat perplexed.

Kemp quickly opened the door allowing the Doctor to enter. Then spoke. "Mohammed, what the hell are you

The Silent Apostle II

doing here? I thought you were supposed to be making preparations for your Doctor Hawas in Cairo, for this week's visit or something, and the how the hell did you know we were here?"

Elfecky clasped his hands and greeted Darlene. "Indeed, I should have contacted you, Kemp, but you are in grave danger. I had to escape Cairo for a few days while my friends take care of some domestic business," he remarked, then explained that an ancient Order of Cairo had somehow heard about the strange goings on in the museum and were convinced that Darlene was some sort of 'living dead' entity and needed to be terminated.

Elfecky explained that the Grand Lodge of Cairo were amongst the Temple's greatest enemies, and had thought their existence expired a long, long, time ago.

"Well, that was up until after you guys left Cairo and I was paid a visit by one Ahmed El Kabbal, of the GloC. He is a very odd sort of man. He even looks quite evil if you ask me, dead from the neck upwards, and hails to represent the afterlife. He is clearly convinced that a time lock had been activated and that Darlene was somehow possessed by an ancient entity from the other side.

But to my real surprise, he had accused me of devil dealings and worshipping Satan, which is absolutely preposterous. He also claims that I was instrumental in this Assignation ritual."

The Professor was clearly upset as Hastings sat him down and provided him with a nice cup of warm Lipton's tea. "Sorry, Mohammed, this is all I can do. Hotels don't cater for everyone's taste I am afraid."

Kemp walked to the window and stared out, then spoke again. "I think we have just met one of the Grand Lodge of Cairo's members, or at least one of their active members. They have just tried to assassinate Darlene, by trying to run her over in broad daylight."

Mohammed stood up and placed a golden amulet in Darlene's hand. "Here, take this amulet, Darlene, this is the lucky eye of RA. It once belonged to the Queen of Sheba, and the Magdalene or your Assignation mummy, or so I am told.

I don't think she will mind now that you have been blessed with the 'Assignation' of the Magdala. It is symbolic of eternal life here on Earth, and should protect you. If you turn it over you will see that it has the same cartouche inscription as your small tattoo on the nape of your neck. I did not want to say too much until I was absolutely clear on what we were dealing with."

Darlene was mesmerised as she took time to contemplate what the good Professor had just said, then took a good long look at the golden jeweled amulet. She then stood up and wiped her face with both hands as she mumbled. "A walking zombie, is that what you have just said to me Mohammed, that these morons of the GLOC think I am some sort of half-life?"

Hastings interrupted her and the Professor. "So what the hell do we do now?" he asked, tapping his finger against the glass pane of the window?

Mohammed sniffed the air then took a drink of his tea. "I don't think their activists could have followed me here, as I travelled under my twin brother's passport. I do that sometimes, so the authorities may think I am still in Cairo, but it won't take long for them to discover I am not at the museum. Darlene needs to travel to this address here in Malta. She must show the Cipher her tattoo, and no-one else. Then we have to wait.

The Cipher originally was known as the unique sword maker from the ancient after world, and possesses the power of scrying, or soothsaying and of which is rumoured in some circles that Ciphers can actually see deep into the future. I am not sure how accurate this information is but I have only one other offering and you certainly won't like it."

Hastings turned and glared his eyes at Mohammed. "If it means hurting Darlene in any shape or form then you can forget it, Moh, as long as I have breath in my body she will be protected."

"Oh, no! My dearest Kemp, you misunderstand, it is the other way round, it's not Darlene that will need protecting, she will most likely end up protecting you," came the odd reply.

"Darlene has the Assignation, remember, she has touched the afterworld, she has been blessed with greatness, she has journey beyond the realms of astral life. The Grand Lodge will not stop trying to kill her until they are assured that she is no longer a threat or until they have her locked away in some dark dungeon somewhere. Or in the worst case scenario send her back into the afterlife with her progenitors where she does not belong."

Hasting's mouth dropped open, and then he muttered the word 'progenitor' over and over. "Are you saying Darlene is actually part of some ancient Royal family lineage? Because if you are, then I think you are so wrong. It was I who chose Darlene to authenticate the 'Sanctos Epistula'. It was me who brought her into this charade in the first place. And now you are saying that I have been manipulated by someone who now wants Darlene dead?"

"Oh, yes!" remarked the Professor quite flippantly, whilst staring at Darlene. "You see the powers of the afterlife move across vast regions indiscriminately. They don't settle in any one part of the cosmos for any length of time. They roam the ethereal plane as astral nomads, and stalk the living to pass on their odd legacy of existence. It's just the way of things.

I would wager that our Darlene here was first removed from her job at the university in a trumped up scenario that left her very vulnerable, and you my friend were activated by the Fisher Kings to find someone with relevant expertise in order to quickly to authenticate the Magdala Epistula before lent. And were perhaps redirected by misdirection or manipulated to obtain Darlene's whereabouts and her availability, then recruit her, of course which you did."

Hastings clenched his fist. "Carter, that little, twisted shit! I will wring his little, fat neck, when I get my hands on him," he muttered, whilst staring again at Darlene. Then rubbed his face. "Darlene, when did Carter actually first contact you?" he asked, flicking his mobile phone open.

She thought for a moment then answered. "Actually, he didn't. It was you who contacted me Kemp, when you first came to my presentation, I did not know who Carter was before then."

Kemp grimaced. "He must have orchestrated this bloody whole thing. Mohammed, where do we find the Cipher? Because if my hunch is correct Darlene may not have much time; the Cipher may be our only hope."

Hastings grabbed his laptop and searched a few web sites, then sent a few emails to some serious people in his working life. The Professor was scribbling a few notes into his notebook, as Hastings planned his next move.

"Mohammed you had better accompany us to Scotland. I think we need to take a break somewhere safe where we cannot be intercepted. We will leave in the morning."

The Professor tapped his gold pen on the note book top. "Sounds like a plan. I need to make some calls."

Chapter Nine
Human Emotion

The church bells at the nearby cathedral, opposite the hotel had started to sing their song to the Lord above. A clutch of white pigeons had taken flight, sending a flutter of white feathers drifting down from the belfry onto the piazza below.

Darlene had lit fourteen candles and set them around the rim of the rustic cast iron bath tub. The tub itself had been built into a huge, oval shaped marble pedestal resembling what Darlene would describe as a Roman dipping pond, but with hot water.

She paused and sniffed the vanilla aroma whilst simultaneously allowing the hot steam to envelop her face. She gazed as the many flames flickered and danced across the water's top. "Mmmmh!" she muttered.

She had littered the top of the water with a range of rose flower petals that had begun displacing themselves almost covering every inch of the surface. The arrangement of colour was white, blue, red and green leaves and left the bath with an aura of brightly lit water and perhaps one of the most welcoming baths she had taken for a while.

Letting her dressing gown slip off her shoulders and fall onto the floor, Darlene stepped into the warm water and immersed herself into her aquatic, heavenly indulgence.

She slowly smoothed lavender soap over her buxom breasts and shoulders then crunched her hair up, just tucking it up enough to clear her neckline. She then smiled as she simply relaxed and lay back into the mass of petals.

Meanwhile, the latch on the front door had clicked several times then fell silent. Across the open living quarters the bathroom door lay ajar, making it possible for Darlene to observe the complete living space. She knew the door had been tried yet she did not stir, she was mindful that the door was unlocked and yet it still never opened, despite having just been tried.

Kemp Hastings had found a new experience in his turbulent life, an experience that he did know how to control or respond to. Although he was a worldly experienced man, he did not know how to react to Darlene at the best of times. His head spun every time she was around him. She made him feel both awkward and strong and yet her vulnerability gave him a sort of responsibility having brought her into this mess.

He tried the door again. Then it opened. On entering the flat, he gazed directly through the room and straight at Darlene who had slid down deeper into the marble Victorian-styled bathing tub.

"Beautiful," he murmured under his breath, taking a lot longer to avert his eyes from her voluptuous body, even more so now that it was covered in fresh bubbles and coloured petals.

He thought for a few moments remembering Dante's Sank Real oil painting that was pivotal in this conundrum. She was as every bit as stunning as Rossetti had imagined. Yet he, the artist would have never observed his model in the modern world, with these complicated Egyptian inflictions or have been bestowed on such a fine female specimen.

Darlene remained silent and still as Kemp's mind wandered off into the heavens contemplating many ways of approaching her, especially now that she was in her naked and perhaps most vulnerable state. He stared again praying that Darlene would not wake, or turn and catch him in his lecherous state of mind, thus preventing any chance of a physical union with this stunning, flaming-red haired lady.

She momentarily sniffed then gave out an almost erotic long sigh. The groan that sent Kemp's blood level racing high up into the red zone of any heart thumping measuring device. He needed to do something quickly; the timing for him was perfect, but how would she respond? Then suddenly, he found himself talking out loud.

"Is there enough room in that tub for two?" he asked. Somehow the words had uncontrollably had made themselves present in the room. He thought he had said those words. But did he? Had he imagined it? Did he actually say those simple words? Had he actually thought them out loud? No, he could not have done so, it was not like him, he was brave but not that brave, or was he far more sensitive than he thought? And besides, he preferred the woman to play first base.

If Darlene had led him on, then he would have been certainly loyal as a puppy dog and remain at her every beg and call, but still, he would not have given it a second thought, nor given in to her womanly charms too easily. But, as far as Darlene was concerned, he would walk over hot coals for her. He just did not know how to tell her.

The water lapped up against the side of the marble ledge sending a single wave rippling over the base of the candles. Darlene's eyes had opened and she was staring back at him. Her mouth was slightly open, her flaming-red hair hung over her shoulders and down onto her left, heaving bosom.

Kemp stared uncontrollably again. Darlene could feel her nipples becoming stiff as she was becoming aroused; the warm waters and the moment had done their trick and had trapped her womanly make up and desires. The moment of emotions had wrapped them up into a single raging ball of pulsating heat.

She knew she had blushed, and she could feel her body starting to pulse away, her heart rate increased a little more and had gone into over load as she turned her gaze away ever so slightly in the water to evade further eye contact, but luckily for her it was too late and she smiled.

Kemp had already taken a seat on the edge of the bath and had started to remove the loose, red strands of hair from her neckline.

"I could spend the rest of my life in there with you," he said, staring into her eyes and smiling. Darlene had melted; she had already succumbed to his charms at least five days ago.

She paused trying to control her emotions then spoke. "Well, if you stay out there, you will leave me lonely for the rest of my life."

She reached out and grabbed his arm, then rubbed her lips slowly over the skin. A single kiss on his hairy wrist followed by a slow tug on his arm and Kemp ended up in the water fully clothed. Neither caring, they were just both intent on satisfying both their lust and desire.

Kemp suddenly leaned forward and grabbed her delicate face with both hands then slowly kissed her lips, she responded by groaning slightly then began gripping his arms as the heat inside her stomach erupted and intensified sending showers of shivers of pulsing warm pleasure through her writhing body.

Her tongue had already found his soft warm lips and was sending tiny sparkles of delight over his face. They both froze in each other's arms enjoying the moment. Darlene had already started to melt like a huge candle under extreme heat; her hands were sweating and jittering uncontrollably as the excitement built up in her womanhood.

Her skin had tightened and her stomach felt as though it was having a great day on a roller coaster at the carnival with a few million butterflies flying in and around in her womb, and yet she was somehow floating in complete ecstasy.

She knew she was panting and she was loving it. Then she moaned again as another shower of warm pulses flashed through her breasts and groin, sending Hastings into a frenzy of kissing and soft dribbling.

Darlene had been overcome by his soft manly charms and good looks. His body aroma was now playing a major role in driving her lustful desires. No matter what Kemp asked her to do, she knew she would openly obey without hesitation. She was captured in his web of 'maledom'.

He removed his shirt, and then slid comfortably next to her in the warm waters taking time to caress her bosom at first, and then he slowly let his tongue drift over her erect nipples on their way down to her pierced belly button. She gave out another warm whimper.

Then she moaned louder as he grabbed her face again and kissed her intently on the soft lips as a man should. She, meanwhile, traced his belly and breast hairs with her long finger nails sending ripples of passion sensations over his chest. He smiled and shuddered but let her continue; she fumbled a bit then gasped as she found his manhood.

She knew now he was not the smallest of men on the planet and the rule or notion that a hand's span and width measured up to the length of a man's penis, supposedly equal to one another which now the theory was confirmed as the myth had just been blown out of the water.

"Mmmm, you must have that thing on steroids," she whispered. Then shifted uneasily in the blanket of bubbles then headed directly for the satin duvet cover at the thought of his manhood tearing at her soft vulnerable skin.

Throughout the course of the evening they lay coupled together in each other's arms, slowly making love several times in all conceivable positions—putting the Karma Sutra into shame as a few new hidden realms of bodily contortions were tried out, especially now as each new change of position was bonding them together as an intimate loving couple.

After two hours, Darlene was abruptly awoken as Hastings could be heard shouting from behind the locked door to the apartment. She soon realised that she had fallen asleep in her bath, and awoke only to acknowledge she had just had one of the best dreams of her life, and yet the man she wanted so much to be with was locked outside the flat trying to get in.

She donned her house coat and let the private investigator back into the hotel room.

"Well, that will certainly have to become a reality," she whispered softly and headed back to the bathing room.

Chapter Ten
The Grand Lodge of Cairo

High on the concrete pedestal, the sign of '**Sophia**' stood elegant and proud, a sign that Baphomet was still an entity being worshipped by the anti-Knights' Templar group—the GloC or The Grand Lodge of Cairo.

To the left of the masonic symbol, sat four etched engravings written in the 'Atbash' Cipher text, a reverse image of what one would conceive as normal Arabic scripture.

Above the apex of the doorway, the reverse logo of mixed symbols was clearly sending an unholy message to those who walked the paths of the dead, and would acknowledge the presence and a definitive indicator of this unholy order was in their midst.

Baphomet, or Sophia, was the dominant name of a well-known Greek Goddess which adorns the main hallway entrance and was a reminder of the Order's struggle against the Holy Order of The Knights' Templar.

Hastings had crossed proverbial swords with this group several times before but they had never tried to kill him or any of his friends before; well, that was up until they had struck out at Darlene recently. If the 'Magdalene' had chosen Darlene as her window of entrance into the 21st century then the GloC was her archetypical glazier; a fanatical society who would be on a mission to smash her existence into a million tiny shards of glass.

The anger from the Goddess of the Gnostics was not one to be taken lightly and every step would have to be carefully thought out and calibrated to exacting detail if they were to survive this potential spate of attacks. And where would Professor Elfecky fit into all this—how could he protect the group?

The GloC or the Sophians would often make reference to their prize possession of which was not disputed by the Templar Order in any shape or form. The argument was to the effect that their most treasured possession was that of an ancient skull, in which they pray and observe devout allegiance to. The Order was convinced that this token was not the head of John the Baptist, but the Sophians believed otherwise.

Hastings thought for a few seconds and gathered his ramblings into one train of thinking: he had received three telephone calls asking if he was the cipher. Could it be that his relationship with the Fisher Kings had crossed paths and meanings, and that they had somehow logged his cell phone somewhere in the wrong domain, and someone was using the signal to locate his whereabouts?

He gazed up and caught an extract that had been cast in stone on the entrance wall:

- Plain: אבגדההוזחטיכלמנסעפפצקרשת
- Cipher: תשרקצפעסנמלכיטחזווהדגבא

Hastings quizzed the simple text. He could not make head nor tail of what he was looking at, but he knew

Darlene could crack the code very quickly. He closed his jacket and made his way into the dark doorway and waited.

Not before long a red Porsche Carrera had parked across the street. He recognised the car immediately. His hunch had been correct, somehow he knew the curator at the Temple at M'dina appeared to be a little aloof and was not too helpful when asked some very simple questions, but Kemp had expected such.

The powers that be were apparently being manipulated by an informal team of dwellers who were not of the direct Knights' Templar Order and were somehow working the Order from within its own ranks. Hastings had his suspicions but would not dare confront the Order head on; he knew that would indeed be literal suicide.

He quizzed his address book in his mobile telephone and clicked a fast call number. "Good afternoon, Major, I need your help. Do you have ten minutes? I wish to discuss the Hellfire Cross Sword with you again."

The Major at the other end of the phone coughed a little, then the phone went suddenly quiet. Then he spoke softly. "Mister Hastings, listen to me very carefully you are in grave danger you need to get out of Cairo soonest. I hear that the Grand Council of Cairo want to seize Darlene, please, Mr Hastings, find somewhere quickly and lie very low. This is a situation of life and death. His holiness the Pope is in the office as we speak.

He is making some ad hoc plans to review our security. It appears that we have found some rather highly technical equipment that can create a 3D super hologram image. We think it was used to project the image of the Hell Fire Sword within our display case number 33. And he said, only this morning, that there is some unholy ripplings in the fabric of our society.

He then asked me to re-open the case of the Sanctus Epistula. We have been very much compromised. We have intercepted a new group who have designs on the Vatican's archive. It has come to light that a small knot of information technology buffs have created a hybrid software package called 'The Archimedes Construct'. It consists of a series of high powered 3D CGI or computer generated images which were used to beam the image of the painting from Rossetti on the wall of the sealed chamber in the gallery.

The other side of the coin is that our own domestic situation here is of grave concern as we have seven Swiss Guard soldiers under lock and key for their deception in the plot to steal the actual Hell Fire Cross Sword.

They had created this Archimedes Construct digital imaging software in its mature state and was designed as a military program, a camera which projects and beams human images over long distances known as a 3D—GPL parametric humanoid, normally employed to project a human form in motion, but in our case was used in the 'still frame program' with no video or motion distortion.

Our Vatican IT specialists say that the program is a multi-layered model using a 'Houdini profile'—whatever that means. So in essence, Mister Hastings, I am all confused with newfangled digital things. But, I do understand that they did not use any software or metadata 3D Modeling programs to create the image of the 'Holy one'. The apparition that had appeared to his Holiness the Pope, as far as we can make out, well, Mister Hastings, this is a bit of a conundrum, she was quite real!

As far as we can tell. And we have no explanation to say otherwise. The Swiss Guard Officers also say that they encountered a grey, phantom monk who was walking within the sealed archive and was looking for the Holy parchment and that he, this 'ghost', had relieved the guards of the real Hellfire Sword, they also say that he just simply disappeared along with it.

That is why I have sent you some complex emails. But beware, my friend, do not trust anyone. And, whatever you do, don't, answer to anyone called the Cipher. This Cipher appears to be this monk. He may be an Arch Angel of Death, Mister Hastings, or he may an Angel of Mercy—we do not know for sure. If the GLoC call you, please check your incoming numbers. They will find you simply by your mobile telephone signal, and let us know soonest if you are contacted, Mister Hastings, the Vatican is at your disposal. May the Lord above be with you."

Hastings had responded by sending a simple text back to Major La Rue at the Vatican. It read: MALTA.

The phone went dead and Hastings could swear that he heard a double tap on the line. He waited and listened: nothing. He then turned off his phone completely, and made his way back the hotel.

Darlene was already in the foyer waiting for the desk clerk to appear, when Kemp suddenly pushed her through the glass door.

"Ah, Darlene, there you are. We need to move out of here. I have booked us on a flight to Scotland. We need to get as far away from here and Cairo as we possibly can. Major La Rue thinks that the Vatican security systems have been tampered with and that the case containing the sword was also a 3D hologram image to deceive the actual cameras.

Darlene smiled. "Did they not check all the electrical equipment after the first breach of their internal security? I recall the Major saying that the only thing that was inconclusive was the image of the entity, and I am sure that was real enough, because there was no way they could beam an image like that into my head let alone into my bathroom, Kemp. Absolutely preposterous to think otherwise."

Kemp looked bewildered, then spoke, still harboring the notion that events were one hundred per cent created by man, and yet somehow the advent of this entity troubled him. "No, but if they could make an image look solid in an art gallery, then perhaps they could even make an image appear real anywhere else. And what I mean by that is Dante's Sank Real oil painting, they made it appear as a real canvas painting, although it was already gone, or more likely stolen."

Hastings presented some thoughts. "What if the painting had been replaced some time ago? Disappeared along with the sword after they took possession of it? That would take more than just a handful of specialists to achieve this level of deception, this sounds very much like a huge cover up. The Major says, that the cameras in the Vatican can be overridden electronically, but to impose an actual 3D picture on a single unit is impossible as several cameras are in each vault.

Well, that's what he thinks. But he did say they have several Swiss Guard soldiers in prison due to their involvement. Anyway all these events would still take some really careful long term planning." Kemp paused for a few seconds then smiled again. "I know that the Rossetti was housed in a sealed case on the wall, and I bet you that some new security system was recently installed, or as recently as six weeks to seven ago. I would wager my next set of car tyres on it."

Darlene looked confused. "Are you saying that these cases are designed to project 3D images onto surfaces within the display cases and could be used to trick the human eye?"

Kemp pursed his lips then spoke. "Not the cases but state of the art micro image projectors that can over-ride or trick the security systems, and these images were projected across the whole Vatican with a range of highly detailed photographs, not just the archive chambers but everywhere, gates, doorways, hallways, kitchens, car parks and even the admin offices themselves.

The complete system was replicated, and here is the scary bit: the software was less than 500 bucks to buy off the internet. Not beyond rational thought, eh! Don't you think there is some very clever electrickery at work here."

Just then the desk clerk appeared. Hastings turned and gazed over the car park, then suddenly grabbed Darlene and huddled her into the emergency stairway. "Darlene sssh, just trust me, we need to go and I mean now, hurry back to the room and pack what you need, we might have about ten minutes if we are lucky. I have just seen what I think are the black Knights of Cairo. Three of them sitting in the blue BMW across the car park, they were at the square and at M'dina earlier today. That means they are most likely watching us."

He then called the front desk to organise a taxi to the airport, and Darlene packed what little clothing she had, and never asked any more questions. She trusted Kemp with her life and he knew he was taking responsibility for her. She would let him take the lead for now and play along with his mad charade campaign.

The private investigator then contacted Mohammed and let him know of their intentions. One hour and forty minutes later the Al Italia plane took off for London Heathrow with the two investigators and one Professor of Egyptian archaeology on board.

Chapter Eleven
The Vatican Responds

Major La Rue sat at his desk and viewed the electronic schematic of the Vatican's entire radiotelephony and internet network. His laptop had been beeping almost non-stop over the past hour as email upon email was sent in response to his one hundred and three requests for answers from the internal IT—Wi-Fi—technical division of the 'Holy See'.

La Rue was perplexed, he was struggling with the notion that twelve members of his trusted Swiss Guard had turned renegade and had been systematically stripping the Vatican of its many riches and he, as a devout soldier and custodian, was hell bent on returning the Vatican back to its absolute status of control whilst deciding on a course of action to restore discipline.

The interior papal administrator had since been removed from office and was now under investigation from the Vatican's serious fraud squad and had been charged with allegations of perverting the course of justice and actual theft from the Papal office. Major La Rue remained mindful that the administrator may not even make it to the court rooms alive—if caught up in the 'murky' politics of Vatican life.

The internal protocols and procedures of the Holy See's internal process was based on a very old and simple principle; it hails from the time of Alexandria the Great, where if a man or woman can muster up more than three persons to corroborate their side of a case or charge, then they are automatically acquitted, or conversely if three or more persons submit the same charge then the perpetrator is automatically dead.

The process today has been made somewhat more complex as any charges raised of wrong doing are managed under the Templar rule of logic. A rule based on fact and truth.

Chapter Twelve
Womanly Charms

After arriving in Scotland, Hastings had planned a further excursion to the island of Iona to escape the GloC—Grand Lodge of Cairo, and had spontaneously arranged a few days rest and recouperation on the small island known as the Isle of Mull, in order to visit an old friend and cleric Dr Colm Cille McDuff.

As he drove to the Chapel at 'Reilig', along with the Professor and his assistant, the trio took time to absorb the beautiful views on display. Scotland's highlands and islands in the north certainly can put other so called country sites of interest to shame. And, as far as Scotland was concerned, her natural ruggedness and unbridled weather was complimentary and a must for any overseas visitor.

McDuff was the strangest cleric Kemp had ever met. His family hailed from all parts of Scotland and he chose to live the life of a recluse not too far from what he says was his family ancestral home on the wee island.

If McDuff was to be believed he would say that he was a direct descendant of St Columba himself. Or his lineage belonged to one of his many close family of followers that remained as a clutch of protectors through the centuries.

Suffice to say the cleric was an absolute fruitcake but, luckily for Kemp, one of the best sources of island knowledge alcohol could buy. After a couple of hours, they arrived at the wee village and found their host. Darlene and the Professor had taken the decision to leave Kemp to his own devices and walked along the sea shoreline, then ventured into the graveyard as Hastings engaged the cleric.

As the cold wind rushed between the grave stones, Mohammed and Darlene Gammay quizzed a few epitaphs looking for the ancient marker graves. Darlene drew her hand along one of the larger stones and stopped.

"Doctor, do you think Kemp is coping well with all this GloC and Vatican stuff?"

The Professor paused for thought then answered. "Miss Gammay, Kemp Hastings is the most capable investigator I have ever had the honour to know. In certain subjects, he can run rings around any scholar, he is a very learned man, but he won't admit it. He likes things to be simple and can apply a rational answer to most things he challenges.

But you can trust me when I say that you are probably his biggest challenge, Darlene, he does not know how to act around you, he somehow feels responsible for you. And yet you are highly capable of looking after yourself, maybe you should tell him how you feel, but be gentle, his emotions are on the boil at the moment."

After his lengthy discussion with the cleric, Darlene and Hastings walked through the old village then for Darlene it was a walk back into the old St Columba chapel. Having reverently wandered between the grave stones both Darlene and Kemp were a little less perplexed and on the front of it, appeared more relaxed as they walked with the grounds of the old cemetery.

"Kemp, I think I really need to change my appearance, before we go back to the city. I was thinking of making my hair really blonde and my eyes a piercing blue and cut my hair into a bob style. What do you think?"

Kemp stopped and stared at her for a few moments. "I think you look fine the way you are Darlene. You are everything and more any man could wish for. I mean look at you, you're intelligent, you're sexy, you possess a good chunk of demure and certainly wilder with the outgoing pursuits than any other woman I have ever encountered.

Any man would be overwhelmed by your high morals and integrity and certainly displaced by your intellect." He suddenly cut himself short, and just knew he had just committed himself to Darlene's armoury of assets as far as men were concerned, but in his case he wanted her to know that he liked her.

"So are you saying you fancy me, after our tete-a-tete?" Then she suddenly realized that their tete-a-tete was not a real physical one, but one her fantasy dream. She realised her emotions were running riot, touching on her fantasy base and of which were now appearing at surface.

Kemp was suddenly in very unfamiliar territory. His heart started pounding again, he could not help staring at her, Darlene still remained hesitant of an answer.

"I suppose what I am saying Darlene is that you are quite beautiful and you could have any man on the planet as your soul mate. I mean just look at you, simply gorgeous."

Darlene blushed then smiled. "Well then, it's a good job you are here with me then for protection. My knight in shining armour to protect me from whatever it is we are actually dealing with. All you need is your Excalibur; I will be your Guinevere," she exclaimed, just as Kemp pushed by and stood in front of her.

Standing at the door of the entrance to the church stood a single monk, clad in an all-grey habit, holding in his hand what Kemp knew was the Vatican's Hellfire Cross Sword. There was no question about it.

"Stay still and do not move, Darlene, this is the creep from the car accident at Restenneth, and if my suspicions are correct he may have also visited the Vatican."

The monk looked up then beckoned the two to follow him back into the small cloister area of the church. Both Darlene and Kemp knew that this was no dream nor any figment of their collective imaginations and they followed the grey-clad cleric into the chapel.

This monk appeared real enough and what frightened the investigators most was that he knew who they both were. They stopped then gave each other a single and nodded, then slowly and very cautiously entered the old chapel. Just as they entered the structure, the heavy wooden doors closed without any assistance, then apparently locked itself.

The monk removed his grey hood exposing his 'nosure' the lack of hair around the central point of his head made Hastings take a moment in time to acknowledge that he was in the presence of a real time ancient cleric of Christ, or that's what he appeared to be.

It was then that the Cleric leaned forward, and spoke. "I see you have met Mister McDuff, then? I keep him here as a deterrent to keep the nosey few out of my complicated affairs."

The monk then walked behind the altar and knelt down. There was a shuffling sound for a few moments then it was very quiet. He then re-appeared and engaged the couple in direct conversation.

"Mister Hastings you are not aware of it yet, but McDuff has had to deal with your Professor friend; do not worry it was quick and very painless, McDuff is excellent with a blade. Your Professor is not who you think he is, he is not Professor Mohammed Elfecky of the University of Egypt, he is or was, Doctor Rashid Abbas Elfecky from the Grand Lodge of Cairo. He was the identical twin brother of your friend Mohammed who passed away seven months ago, your friend died from a chronic ulcer in his lower intestine.

He was however, very instrumental in keeping this sword in very safe keeping. Sadly the sword should have never ever have been returned to the Holy Vatican under any circumstances. But the GloC well, suffice to say that they 'the anti-order' had taken some strange steps to upset the balance of things.

They had hypnotized your good Dr Mohammed Elfecky and had migrated his working thoughts to their pseudo Dr Elfecky here, as far you are concerned Rashid and his brother Mohammed were one of the same person.

The hidden power of these archaic mind-melding techniques are very much still used today a lot more frequently as you would like to think, Mister Hastings. The GloC were aware that an 'Assignation' was due and that they had orchestrated many events to try and capture assignees as they pass to and from the afterlife.

Luckily, for your Miss Gammay, I was there to keep the under-Lords at the other side of the gateway using the

Hellfire Cross Sword, but that was only for a limited time, but let us discuss something that neither of you would have contemplated in any detail, and that is your joint role in your Assignations to the ethereal plane."

Hastings stepped forward and stood directly in front of Darlene. "I will not let you harm a single hair on her head, and I don't care where you are from, we have been through a virtual hell and if you think you can frighten us then think again. Cleric."

Hastings was slowly moving toward the monk who smiled and observed Hastings anger coming to surface. He then stopped momentarily as Darlene eased slightly forward towards him, if Darlene possessed a secret so potent that it displaced him, then he was suddenly vulnerable and changed his line of conversation.

"My dearest friends, I am actually here to protect you, not to harm you? Am I here to employ you? Yes. I have indeed travelled here to your planet but only to arm you both with great wisdom and knowledge.

You see, you are my succession, you each possess qualities that we of the afterlife require, and you are both assignees."

The monk stopped rambling and returned behind the altar then bent down again.

Chapter Thirteen
Tartarus Inferni

Outside in the bone yard a blue, greyish mist had appeared and swirled up across a single gravestone; an epitaph marker stone that was situated centrally in the marble clad aisle, embedded amongst the myriad of testaments of existence to the dear and departed, albeit, this stone had no writing, just an effigy or carving of the infamous and legendary 'Green Man'.

This mist was however no ordinary run-of-the-mill spectre, this entity was something entirely different, this was the mother of all demons, this visitor was Death himself.

After a few minutes the mist in the bone yard had cleared and standing fully upright at 7 foot 2 inches in height, clad in a mix of black and deep burgundy coloured robes, stood the 'Grimmest of Reapers' in all his deathly glory.

His sullen gaze was scanning death's body park, the bony remains of the interred quietly lying at rest, each calcium corpse peaceful in demise. Death's odd gaze scanned the cemetery. It was as if he was looking for a specific, offending corpse or a lost soul in particular. He was searching for an entity that may have fallen off the hard beaten path into the river Styx.

"Mmmmmm!" rang a deep, single tone as the sound bite resonated across the churchyard causing each chunk of stone to vibrate slightly in its foundations; each epitaph having been struck by the un-heavenly voice of demise. High above and touching the skies, the huge, metal cruciform of the cross was sitting on top of the apex of the high spire and rang out a single 'C' sharp note as it vibrated in unison with the cruet set as it sat laid out for all to see on the altar top down below.

Death was searching for something important; he knew not what exactly! Nor exactly where it was! But he was aware that a single article of faith was somewhere in his domain, and he was to say the least very concerned as to its whereabouts, and its earthly custodian.

Meanwhile, in the small Abbey the Cistercian Monk stood next to the granite altar stone and laid the heavy, golden sword reverently onto the altar top, with its long silver and very sharp blade pointing to the east. He dropped his hands by his side then spoke.

'Sit, please and don't make a single sound. As long as we have this Hellfire Cross Sword here with us, Death will stay at arm's length, but he has very keen hearing," he said, pointing to the doorway at the far end of the chapel.

"We are under the protection of a particular God, one could say, your God actually Miss Gammay but not your God, Mr Hastings, you have a very different path to follow." Hastings was amused by the strange comment. "I am the Cipher, some call me 'The Dream Weaver' others call me 'Intrusive', but I like to think of myself as the provider of knowledge, and I can assure you both my intentions are always for good purpose. And as they say, one cannot make an omelet without slaughtering a few potential chickens in the process, and that's the difficult bit, keeping the balance of right and wrong.

My Earth name is Kyle Wishart and as you may have already deduced I do not belong to this world. I am a free roaming entity with perhaps more of a substantial physical presence, unlike the other entities you have been exposed to recently, they are simple apparitions, they are figments of fragments of time pulses, not really harmful or fully developed, but can play with the human psyche and heart strings on occasions. I am however very different. I am a traveler in time."

The Cipher stopped talking and stared into Darlene Gammay's eyes, then smirked.

"And you, Miss Gammay, are also certainly very different. Although you are not aware of the consequences completely as yet, but you have had a valuable insight into the magical afterlife, a glimpse into a world that mortal man does not exist, nor can.

You have seen and witnessed more than any other mortal living soul on this planet ever has. You, my dear lady, have been very unlucky or lucky depending on your outlook as you have been singled out by the most unusual of circumstances, followed by some 'momentous events' that are even very far-fetched for normal 21st century thinking. But, when we delve back in time several thousand years or so, you are placed right deep in the thick of it all.

But recently some things on the elemental level have changed since your last visit, and that is why I am here. I am the current custodian of the Hellfire Cross Sword, or the 'Tartarus Inferni'. It's awesome, destructive power must be harnessed at all times, and that's why the 'Grimmest of Reapers' will not dare step foot in this holy place. He dare not—whilst this article of faith remains in this domain.

This God killing sword is the last instrument of protection for your humankind on this planet. The blade wields potency so powerful that even the grand masters of the heavens don't dare intervene with its existence.

They are all far too afraid to get involved or wrapped up in astral politics, as this sword has brought down many ancient gods and goddesses in its life time. And, I have a duty to pass on custody of such an unearthly weapon to a worthy custodian.

Just then, Darlene's eyes lit up with something that resembled almost pain or pleasure, she was not quite sure which it was, but squirmed on the pew as she adjusted her seating position thinking about the concept of possessing such a weapon.

Kemp, meanwhile, sat quietly with his head slightly lowered almost in prayer, and was listening intently. The monk took a single step down from the altar staging as Kemp looked up.

Brother Hastings permit me to explain a few things to you: it was I, who stood in front of your car near the Priory, it was I, who sent the curator from the museum to Malta to warn you of the Grand Lodge of Cairo, It is I who protect the bones and relics of the holy one, and it was I, who brought the 'Sanctos Epistula' manuscript into existence on behalf of my keeper.

But trust me, when I say that these are all real time events, and there still exists some very real threats to both of your lives. The last Custodian of the Magdalena manuscript was indeed the artist, Gabriel Dante Rossetti.

The Silent Apostle II

It was given to him in the early 19th century by my predecessor, and Dante, the fool that he was, went to extraordinary lengths to uncover its true and potent dark secret powers and did indeed capture the actual face of the Magdalena in his abilities to paint, as did other artists, but not as clearly as Rossetti did.

But, Rossetti a genius by any description, and through his social awareness and understanding of illicit drugs and alcohol had managed to penetrate time and space whilst being consumed in his unique world driven by a heady mixture of Victorian hallucinogenic drugs. This concoction provided him with an unearthly stimulation to his fertile mind, and, he was able to set his mind and soul totally free. And, he did, on several occasions, but he also managed somehow to look into the world that mortal man should fear, or visit a place where heavenly angels should fear to tread.

But sadly contributed greatly to his own demise, he sketched his magnificent portrait of the Magdalena onto a beautifully clean and unblemished church blessed canvas. His artistry in this man and the given subject matter which was painted to such perfection that the real image was spiritually exported from an ancient vellum manuscript and onto this new living modern platform, or your living skin tissue miss Gammay, and, ultimately transported the image from the face of the mummy housed in the Cairo museum of antiquities to you the new host.

This is not the first time either. The curator Mohammed Elfecky, he is what we call an 'alter ego cipher', he is the protector of the mummy here on earth and himself a brother of the Fisher Kings.

But before you two arrived on this planet there were several other 'chosen' to be the face of the Magdalena on earth. There are other events to consider perhaps the face of the Baptist, or Francis of Assisi the one who carried the wounds of Christ as given to him by the Apostle John.

And Bernadette Sobiros, your so called Lady of Lourdes, she spent several days conversing with the holy lady who has rose petals upon her feet, both chosen for their ability to see beyond the normal spectrum of your earthly light.

Custodians such as these generally emerge from these blessings as normal sane people, but modern DNA has somehow infected the process of 'Assignation' and your kind, your so called evolved modern breed, well, they have suddenly become super human against infection or disease.

Their physical beings or their human composition will simply just not erode. Let me tell you that there are, 'one hundred and four' mortal corpses that adorn the many bone yards and cemeteries on this planet. But today, Miss Gammay, you are of a perfect twin sister quality of DNA replication you are as close as any human could ever be to the Apostle's Apostle."

Take Assisi as an example, in that simple little village, no less than seven Saints have emerged from it's population, Seven potential candidates for 'Assignation' and the closest we came to was Saint Francis himself, he was almost one hundred per cent cleansed, but the process was rejected at a very late stage, similarly with other Saints and the young Lady of Lourdes she too came so close to the 'Assignation'

There were others that showed promise, Agnes of Assisi, Clare, Gabriel Lady of Sorrows, Rufinus, Vitalis and Sylvester, all came so close. But you Miss Darlene you are DNA perfect you are the embodiment of our cause, the core of our being, and simply put you are our purest Assignee.

An acute level of confusion and slight tension between the three had manifested itself, just as Kemp stared back at Darlene with a huge smile on his smug face. She nodded again as Wishart walked slowly across to Darlene and touched her cheek with his pinky finger on his left hand, then stroked her cute little nose with his thumb. He then carried on explaining his role in God's playpen.

"My basic duty a few days back was to place all unearthly things back into a certain order, purely for continuity of process. But in that interim period, Darlene, you had somehow inadvertently or deliberately touched the 'Sanctos Epistula' the letters of the Saints, and triggered yet another transition phase that created a blip in spiritual continuity, you were gifted with etheric vision, this is a blessing or a talent where you only can see between two different dimensions, a glimpse of two ancient worlds but, in your time and space, and now somehow you saw the afterlife.

Therefore, I had to place you and Kemp somewhere safe, a place where I could get access to you both very quickly, and without too much fuss, and look here you both are. And before you ask. I do have the original Sank Real portrait from that infernal gallery.

Miss Gammay, you should also have a similar portrait I assume? And you can trust me when I say it is absolutely identical to the original, not even Rossetti himself could tell the difference."

Darlene gazed upwards. "I do have it, it is tucked up safely in my apartment under my bed."

Kemp suddenly interjected. "You hid a twenty million pound painting under your bed? What were you thinking girl?" Darlene turned and shot Hastings the most serious of facial expressions that Kemp knew then just when to shut up.

He pursed his lips and grabbed her hand, then gave it a gentle squeeze.

"Sorry, if this is so important, then we need to get custody of it soonest."

The Monk placed a hand on Darlene's shoulder then spoke. Hastings automatically stood back, the presence of this monk just made him very uneasy. "Don't worry about the artwork. We have the oil painting securely back in the afterworld. But sadly you and Mr Hastings, well, we had to arrange an event that would exit you both from society.

And fortunately for you both it was sad that you were hypothetically caught up in the most dreadful and horrendous of fires, and sadly the intensity of which, engulfed your complete house and your poor charred bodies, everything was burned to tiny cinders as the structure of your home, Darlene, was burned to the ground—fuelled by the fires of hell."

Darlene's mouth momentarily dropped open. Then started to shake her head in disbelief. "But what about all my wordly my belongings, all my personal things, my study papers my antiques collection." She turned and gazed at Kemp who could only reach out to console her.

Wishart took a deep breath then spoke again. "Darlene, Kemp, if we did not act in this way then the Black Order—The Grand Lodge of Cairo—would simply hunt you down like a pair of rabid dogs and kill you both.

You have much more serious entities to deal with than just some deranged Druids. But we have been clever and

The Silent Apostle II

have retrieved a lot of things we thought were important for your future life.

The GloC are hell bent on stopping you, Miss Gammay, from basically informing the world at large, that there is a middle gateway twixt the river Styx and your Mother Earth.

This can be very easily corroborated with a series of Egyptian myths and legends which cannot be dismissed, as they are fuelled with truth, these events have indeed actually occurred, and our faith is as real today as it was five thousand years ago.

People want to keep secrets; secrets and one more human death is insignificant in their eyes. This way they will simply stop searching for you two as they will think that you are both dead. One cannot just open a time gateway a couple of times then just stop opening it up, the ancient world of Earth would be over populated by people like me. We are time keepers, and we must strike a sensitive balance of things whilst keeping the time gates alive and aligned.

But we cannot achieve this with your human kind around in existence, your genetic groups. They keep affecting change, you, they keep tampering with time and space, a fault in your drive for knowledge and enlightenment, there is simply too much information around and it is becoming very dangerous."

Kemp spoke up. "So what do you want from us now, then?" he asked.

Clasping his hands the monk Wishart took a step backwards toward the altar then spoke. "I need several things to happen to bring events up to contemporary control, but firstly, trust me when I say Death is already stalking your world with the demise of the human race at the top of his agenda.

The Grim Reaper is on a blood driven rampage. He is searching for your direct progenitors Miss Gammay, he is after your DNA lineage, your line if existence, it is because you are the second line of descendant from Christ, Mary and Joseph of Arimathea.

The Soul collector wants that lineage terminated. Death is trying to reconcile history, he wants you out of the way, and we have strategically intervened and placed the Hellfire Cross Sword in existence, a move to dispel him from showing any interest in the custodians of such a weapon. As I have said, Death will not hang around where this sword is located! Death does not like it; he fears its very existence! He will not remain within fifty feet of its location. You may catch him on the periphery of your vision, but for him that's close enough. So logic says make one of you a custodian of the Hellfire or to be tuned to it's harmonics at any time.

Another thing we must consider is your new identities. Doctor Gammay, I think blonde is a good colour for you. Mister Hastings, not sure what we are going to do with you; you will have to decide how you want to look in the future.

Anyway, for now, come, and let me show you what I mean, and whilst we are at it, let me tell you about or leverage, disguises and costume we can discuss later.

This sword is this steel blade that once belonged to the Emperor Constantine. Then it was acquired by the Great Charlemagne himself who had it molded into the actual sword and had embedded a nail from the crucifixion within its actual configuration. Let's face it, any article that has touched the Holy body of Christ will undoubtedly hail great properties.

Even the Templars during the early crusades used this amazing instrument at Antioch, whilst fighting the infidel, they were granted a vision of where the Holy sword in its earlier configuration lay. Actually, it was me who showed the monk where to find the Holy sword and told them to venture forth and reign over your enemies. The enemy being controlled by Satan himself."

Confrontation;

Wishart retrieved the sword and made his way toward the huge set of oak doors that led out into the Chapel courtyard. Holding the sword aloft, he opened the door. And it was then, as the huge door swung open, a massive black misty cloak of darkness in the shape of a face was caught unawares, and almost appeared to have been startled by the sudden movement of the door and pulled back very quickly.

What stood before them in the graveyard was something that even Wishart himself had not anticipated. Death had resurrected every unearthly soul in the ancient boneyard, two hundred black mist spectres each hovering over their respective graves and gazed back blankly at the Abbey's entrance way.

'This should be interesting.' He exclaimed and grasped the heft of the sword with both hands. Wishart then lowered the sword just as Death began to come forward out from the dense clouds before them. Death then hovered motionless in front of the trio, then hummed another set of very deep haunting tones.

"My children just want you to know or understand what you are up to Wishart. And they are waiting to hear your answer."

Wishart tapped the sword once into the concrete step without any warning, sending a single acoustic pulse across the churchyard, the visible ring of power could be seen rippling through each stone epitaph and up into each entity as it hovered with no intent on doing much, apart from looking dangerous and intimidating.

After a few seconds, the pulse had sent all the souls into a sudden, frightened panic stricken frenzy, and they began flying all over the boneyard, eventually ending up with each soul returning to its respective grave, and returning the sleepy clutch of ghosts to almost serenity. That was apart from Mister Death himself—he was not amused.

The Reaper was still hanging around, and was intending to hang around for a quite a while or so it seemed. It was then that Wishart grabbed the sword handle and spun the pommel piece or end stud of the sword at the hilt and waited.

Death's big, yellow and red eyes instantly widened as he realised that the 'apple' was the end cap of the holiest of articles, and he was gone in a hail of wind and whistle. Wishart screwed the apple back into the hilt.

"And that folks is how we deal with Death. Now, Mister Hastings, you must be very careful when you raise the sword higher than your head, she is very sharp, and very heavy although it is quite fragile, but once you have had some practice with it you will be fine."

Wishart offered the steel to Hastings as he stood awestruck at what had just occurred.

Kemp Hastings reached out then took the 'Tartarus Inferni' sword in his left hand and raised it aloft just as Kyle Wishart disappeared out of view in a cloud of dust.

Hastings stopped gazing upwards then lowered the sword and walked toward the altar. He stopped and faced Darlene. He appeared to have had no choice in his new role and quickly took on the mantle of custodian of this unique God killing sword.

But his instant thoughts were drawn straight back to 5th century Briton, when life was cheap and unruly Kings were raping the nation of their wealth, and the Celtic folklore and mystery of the most famous sword on the planet 'Excalibur' was brought into existence to stem their unholy greed for wealth and power.

He wondered whether or not this was the same killing instrument that had been passed up through the ages, and how many Kings and Queens and unwanted tyrants had it despatched to the river Styx in the heavens, and now it appears to have evolved into the 21st century.

Darlene Gammay watched on as Kemp slowly lowered the sword and placed it by his side then casually walked back into the chapel and laid the sword flat back on the altar top.

"So, Doctor, I believe the sword is recharging itself? What do you make of that?" he asked, then sat down on the cold stone floor.

Darlene stepped up to the altar and was about to lift the sword when it slid across the altar top to a point just beyond the reach of her womanly grasp. She stepped back and gazed towards Hastings; he had not moved an inch or appeared to be remotely concerned.

"Hell's inferno Kemp, did you see that, the sword, it moved, that sword actually just slid across the altar top—look! That is really bizarre, strange even, mind you, then again what we have been through the past few weeks has certainly been far more than just bizarre, whatever next?"

Darlene moved slowly toward the investigator as he sat with his head coupled in his hands. Then she spoke very softly. "Look at us? We are a fine couple of misfits are we not. Me with this damned tattoo and you with your big new knife . . . what have we done to deserve these curses being bestowed upon us? Tell me what did the Apostles say?" she asked expectant of an answer.

Hastings slowly turned around and beckoned her to sit down beside him. After a few seconds they were both sitting, staring at the huge set of oak doors in front of them.

Hastings took a deep breath then spoke. "Well, young lady I am not really that sure, it appears to me that we both have been singled out for some higher purpose in life, we certainly cannot argue about that, but, you know what I really think deep down, I believe that this whole charade was just a cosmic scheme to bring us together. What do you think?"

Darlene clasped both of his hands and placed her head on his shoulder. That was the actual point when the couple clicked and became aware that the cloister's area of the church had begun filling up with a light blue gaseous misty haze that had somehow engulfed the altar and the complete choir area.

The smell of rosewood suddenly filled the Nave as a warm wind spread through the chapel in a swirling fashion.

There was an echo of angels singing somewhere in the back of the House of God, just as the rows of candles suddenly began to light in sequence one at a time, but with no physical intervention, each candle pulsing into life, the sequence running from the main lectern and onto the four main and central gold candle standards that sat adjacent to the effigy of Christ. Then they mysteriously transferred their flame onto the two, large white candles that sat either end of the altar.

Hastings and Gammay stood by and watched in amazement as the church evolved into something more of a huge cathedral than a rural chapel. Darlene spoke softly and watched as the illumination of candles ensued.

"Oh my goodness, Kemp, I have certainly seen this before, remember, I told you that in my bathroom a vision appeared. Well, hang on because, here she comes again . . ." She cut herself short as a flurry of sparks erupted from the altar top and cascaded into the brightly lit church.

After only a couple of short minutes, one hundred and forty candles lit up the inner choir area of the wee chapel of St Columba. Darlene and Hastings moved closer to one another then watched as a succession of 'entities' appeared one by one and stood in a line by a range of pews which ran along the length of back wall of the wooden choir area.

Eleven figures—and eleven angels—stood in silence and gazed upon the couple who moved slowly backwards towards the sacristy doorway. Both humans were embroiled in a state of conscious thought. Hastings accepted that each figure appeared to be a solid person, not an apparition or a ghostly form as was the entities hovering above and behind them, as before, but a physical presence made of flesh and bone.

A few moments had passed when one figure stood up; Darlene recognised this figure as the Apostle Paul. Then he was followed by the other Apostles, each in succession and were holding a single, golden chalice with their names heavily embossed in red lettering upon its jewelled surface.

The tallest of the assembly, John, smiled, then muttered the names of his biblical colleagues. "May I introduce my colleagues in life and my brothers in death: Mathew, Mark, Luke, Acts, Thomas, Thaddeus, Andrew, Mathias, Bartholomew and James."

Behind the assembled 'knot' of phantom Apostles, a single apparition of a woman had appeared and was waving her arms very slowly from left to right across her body. She was still holding a basket of white roses, and she was indeed a very beautiful, angelic figure of a woman—her skin was whiter than white, her eyes bluer than blue, and her fragrance an overwhelming aromatic fragrance of rose water.

Her mass of flowing red hair, which matched Darlene's own colour, appeared softer and livelier and was cascading down over her shoulders and onto her bosom. The medieval white-robed figure cast her right hand over the assembled eleven, white-clad individuals then she spoke very softly. "These are the storytellers, their words are my words, these prophets are my prophets. And they are now yours, your words will be their words and the Lord will know all."

The lady stared on as Darlene reached out somehow to try and touch her, but she was not there and yet she was. The entity smiled.

"Who are you, my lady? Why have you come here to us again?" Darlene asked, then waited patiently for an answer.

The white lady smiled a smile beyond all smiles and blinked her big, blue eyes. "You have been chosen to carry the gospel of the 'one', for I am the Silent Apostle, a consort of Jesus and Apostle to Andrew, for I am the twelfth Apostle and perhaps deemed the Apostles' Apostle, for I am Miriam, the lady of Magda, Princess of the afterlife," she said, then turned to face her collective Saints and Apostles in Arms.

Hastings had dropped his head and was now somehow heavily in deep prayer. He felt a sudden urge not to stare directly at the beautiful maiden. He felt that he was not worthy to gaze upon the righteous, and he was not worthy as a male to gaze upon the face of the Magdalene.

Then the angelic singing had started to get louder and louder and had subtly changed from female voices to a boys' choir of voices, then each pitched so heavenly, as it began hailing a series of louder and higher pitches, certain tones that could literally burst the human inner ear, but the assembled audience were protected from harm.

Then, the entity of the Magdalene floated toward a single statue and took a position at the feet of the porcelain Magdalene figurine. The stone statue stood over ten feet in height and sat on a huge octagonal plinth. The stonework adorned the altar wall of the small chapel.

The Holy entity began swaying from left to right as if becoming totally immersed in something alien to the scene that was literally unfolding before the assembled group of people and phantoms.

Hastings found himself being drawn toward the stained glass window at the east end of the chapel and watched as the face that once dominated Darlene's back and shoulder began to slowly appear on the window glass, it appeared as an etched silhouette on the colourful glass.

To his total amazement the visiting spectre shared the same face as the glass image. Hastings was suddenly very numb. Darlene appeared to be as calm as ever and was staring directly at the beautiful face of the holiest of holy.

The Magdalene turned and smiled, then addressed her attentions toward Darlene directly. Although she appeared to be conversing with her, Kemp Hastings could

The Silent Apostle II

hear no dialogue—in fact he could hear nothing at all for he was totally deaf.

Darlene stared and watched as the Magdalene's lips conveyed her holy words. "My Apostles have laid my path to the new world. The afterlife is a quieter place for now, you have served me well. You will be rewarded with eternal peace and be granted with child, this is my token of love and thanks to you, this child will have a significant royal standing one day."

Another warm breeze slowly swept across the cloisters and Hastings could hear again, but this time it was Darlene who had become deaf as she stood and watched as the twelve Apostles formed a circle of bodies around the figure of Kemp Hastings. Each man appearing to engage the religious investigator in conversation. After a few moments, the Apostles had simply merged into one figure and vanished into the altar top in a haze of blue mist and sparks.

The Magdalene meanwhile, was spreading thousands upon thousands of rose petal leaves across the abbey flooring; a blanket of roses creating, a carpet of flora was spreading out in front of her as she walked down the aisle. She passed by both Kemp and Darlene, turned slightly and smiled at the couple, then disappeared as quickly as she had materialised.

Another great thrust of wind swept through the house of God and the candles were extinguished. The chapel was quiet and the air was slightly colder. Hastings walked backwards to the altar and picked up the sword then stood next to Darlene Gammay.

Darlene was taking deep breaths and wiping her brow. She had become overwhelmed with emotions, and had streams of tears running down her face. She started to talk through her soft weeping. "I really have no idea Kemp, but I feel so relieved, and I have no idea what has just occurred, but I do know that I have been through hell's half acre and back again, and I am too tired, too weak.

I am glad that the return of the Sanctus Epistula is back with its rightful owner—which is good news and the beloved face of Magdalena is back in it's rightful location and returned to its rightful owner in Cairo, but they are one of the same. But this sword thing, well, from what we have just witnessed, well . . . I am certainly confused, the Magdalene, she says . . ." She decided to cut off her speech at that point and waited for Hastings to talk.

She watched as Hastings rubbed the handle of the Hellfire Cross Sword and spoke, "Do not tell me, Darlene, I do not need to know your enlightenment spoken by the Magdalene in her astral tongue—it will not make any sense to me anyway, as will my own revelation from the Apostles will to you. It will all sound like total gobbledygook. Their heavenly tones have been encrypted only to your understanding,and was tuned to our ears only.

It is known as the language of the Apostles or the 'Sanctus Illuminati Verbati'—a hidden esoteric set of rhythms that are tuned to your specific DNA. All very complex stuff I am afraid, and you a scholar too. But, I think we have to go out into the big, wild world and face our fears, my fair maiden.

We must confront the demons that stalk our wonderful world and send them back to Hades, and we have the powerful 'Lancea Longini,' or this 'spear of destiny to assist us. And, hey, we have some very powerful ethereal biblical back-up at our disposal.

This Hellfire Cross Sword to assist us for good purpose, and yet I think we do not even have to have the weapon nearby us, well, that is according to St Paul and the boys, and in honesty, who the hell am I to argue with the Apostles?"

At that moment a whirlwind of dust had emerged from nowhere, then in the blink of an eye, two very distinct figures stood before the couple. Each just staring at one another, Rossetti, was first to speak.

'I see you made it then, much better for one to be illuminated than reflected in a mirror.' He cut off and glanced at his ethereal partner, Bernadette Sobiros blinked her eyes very slowly and smiled.

'Our time to move on has come, you have the mantle of succession, choose your successors carefully, but keep their life cycles within a one hundred years time frame or you lose the DNA signature, peace be with you both.' then nodded reverently.

Before either Darlene or Kemp could respond the whirlwind of dust had engulfed the two and they were gone . . .

Hastings and Gammay both then slowly made their way out of the sacred church, and as they reached the huge Oak doors that momentarily and very much just swung open and without any physical intervention to reveal that the world beyond was a much quieter place.

There were no demons, no spirits, loitering around with menacing intentions, no sign of death himself to confront them, it was just a quiet, lazy cemetery that stretched out before them—just the way bone yards are generally designed to be.

Hastings was first to speak. "I think this Spear of Charlemagne has done it's job.

I don't feel threatened anymore, do you?" he said, just as Darlene stopped in her tracks and gazed up at the sky and smiled a lovely smile toward the heavens above.

She gazed in wonderment as the sun had already risen to it's zenith and the warmth and comforting rays caressed her soft skin in waves of pleasure. She felt her face tingle in the sunlight, and felt good inside in a very odd sort of spiritual way.

Hastings turned and faced Darlene and grasped her left hand, she smiled and blinked those piercing eyes, then shook her head slowly whilst brushing her hair away from her neckline.

They had both endured so much anger, pain, emotional turmoil and now, they had to find a certain reality in their new world of investigative pursuits. Hastings closed the gate to the Kirk behind him and momentarily stopped, then spoke.

Revelation:

"Wait a minute though. I have something to do first," he said, then walked back into the street of the dead, and found a single grave that sat adjacent to the 'Green Man' epitaph. The stone had no name and no writing etched upon it's surface. It was just a headstone with a single rose clearly etched into its front panel.

It was then that he recalled the 'original' Latin text that had been written in the ancient Deunos inscription. It read:

Absconditus, ac adepto admonition angelus.
Concealed at the statue in the Abbey within

a coffin is the important church letter of Magdalene.

The Angel to obtain divine doctrine, I say deceitful warning, sign at the grave is squared. Fear the Church, stand in the highest part, then commit oneself, in silence, this is of great importance. The table of my lineage and testimony of Magdalene.

To carry in front of the Tartarus Inferni—Hellfire Sword and deposit in my holy grave.

Now Hastings was able to decipher the information that had been troubling him since the advent of this strange, yet wonderful experience. Darlene would certainly not have agreed but she was now more subdued and a very much more a wiser woman; albeit, she had endured what can only be described as a biblical phenomenon event.

Hastings was reciting the Latin text out loud and was making simple but rational points as he filtered each line in successive order. "In the abbey interred in a grave, of course, that was the resting place of the Magdalene, which was now not a million miles away.

The manuscript of the saints, well, that was clearly now etched into a stained glass window in the Chapel on Iona, and was ironically painted by Rossetti, who also dabbled in magic. The parchment is now secured in no particular grave per se. The angel had delivered this unique doctrine, not an angel of Christendom but an angel from the afterlife, in the form of an ancient, mummified entity.

The sign and warning of the 'square' most certainly pointed to the Grand Lodge of Cairo, and being on the square as any freemasonry ritual of the modern day will clearly depict, and the base dimensions of the pyramid, well, that was easy for Hastings to work out. It was easily a square based on an octagonal foundation.

The next line read: And to fear the Church is to prostate oneself in prayer and ask for guidance and forgiveness.

The Holy lineage of the Ancient nomads and the people of 'Magdal' have indicated that Mary Magdalene was most certainly a Princess for some and a Queen for others in her own right and of course she crossed into the world of Christendom, and was anointed by Christ but appointed by her peers as the Apostle's Apostle.

Hastings thought for a few more moments longer and toggled with the Latin portion of the final transcript. He was now the custodian of the Hellfire Cross Sword, and for this brief moment in time he was probably the most powerful human being on the planet of Earth. Esoterically, he had become a 21st century 'Thor figure'.

The words: 'Deposit in my Holy grave' echoed in the back of his mind as the final stages of illumination struck home. He waited and began murmuring whilst raising the Hellfire sword above his head, then, with all his strength he drove the steel blade deep into the bowels of the soft sands of the gravesite, and waited.

After a few brief moments, he could feel the sword physically being pulled downwards and absorbed into the soft mud and was literally being torn out of his grasp.

He knew that the sword was designed to 'protect' the holiest of relics and where else better to be, but with the holy steel's rightful owner?

As he watched and waited, he would swear that the headstone was suddenly embossed with an identical carving of the sword, just where the etched picture was placed in a juxtaposition near to the Agnus Dei—Lamb of God icon.

Then a face appeared on the grave stone, it belonged to Mary Magdalene herself. "I thought that was where you belonged," he whispered, then made his way back to find Darlene who had walked a little bit further down the beaten track to death's doorway and was busy sniffing the sweet scent of the red and white roses that adorned the long colourful embankment.

Then she paused and spoke. "Kemp, I can see the angels and cherubs dancing within the mists over here, and over there I see a multitude of fairy queens and nymphs there are thousands of them, you know what though, I always thought they existed—now I know for sure."

The end.

Afterword

There is an unexplained phenomena within the Catholic and Eastern Orthodox Churches known as 'Incorruptibility' and one that simply cannot be explained as the normal breakdown of human tissues is either slowed dramatically down or stemmed completely over a protracted period of time.

It is not to say that decomposition of a corpse does not fully occur, but for this narrative the evidence through study of Bernadette Sobirous's short life was quite compelling as to some of the bizarre circumstances that also surround the subject matter in question.

The author acknowledges that where the simple decomposition of a clinically 'dead' animal or person can, and has defied logic, and that the natural breakdown of a body in some cases perhaps does require further medical investigation and perhaps deeper scientific research.

The author has been stunned by the multitude of such events globally and is cognisant that even in the 21st century there exists some inexplicable occurrences that defy medical science, and the subject of 'Incorruptibility' being one of them.

As the author of 'The Silent Apostle' the subject matter of 'Stigmata' came into question and a subject that can be observed as a living phenomenon in our own life time. There are many casualties of Christ and followers of religious belief who may have a hidden side of their personality or character, and if by stretching our collective imagination a little further—we could argue that these individuals may or could carry an inbuilt 'genetic code' that triggers the advent of the wounds of Christ at a given age, or similarly carry the DNA code of another person who had been crucified or brutally tortured in our violent and turbulent age.

The author wishes to leave you with one thought;

'Although women were at some point in ancient history also crucified' uncommon but actually occurred, and generally, as part of domestic slaves that were from time to time executed under Roman law, an example being from under the Rule of Tiberius where after the death or murder of Tacitus by a slave, the complete domestic staff were executed by crucifixion.

Could we argue that the 'Stigmata' resulting from a female crucifixion, could manifest itself in the modern today?

Made in the USA
San Bernardino, CA
08 January 2013